monster

ALSO BY WALTER DEAN MYERS

FICTION

THE MOUSE RAP

THE RIGHTEOUS REVENGE
OF ARTEMIS BONNER

SCORPIONS
A 1989 Newbery Honor Book

THE STORY OF THE THREE KINGDOMS

NONFICTION

ANGEL TO ANGEL:
A Mother's Gift of Love

BROWN ANGELS:
An Album of Pictures and Verse

GLORIOUS ANGELS:
A Celebration of Children

NOW IS YOUR TIME!:
The African-American Struggle for Freedom

WALTER DEAN MYERS

Monster

Illustrations by
Christopher Myers

WITHDRAWN

■ HARPERCOLLINS*PUBLISHERS*

To John Brendel
for his long friendship

Monster
Text copyright © 1999 by Walter Dean Myers
Illustrations copyright © 1999 by Christopher Myers

For information
address HarperCollins Children's Books, a division of HarperCollins
Publishers, 195 Broadway, New York, NY 10007, or visit our
web site at http://www.harperchildrens.com.

Library of Congress Cataloging-in-Publication Data
Myers, Walter Dean, date
    Monster / Walter Dean Myers ; illustrations by Christopher
Myers.
        p.   cm.
    Summary: While on trial as an accomplice to a murder, sixteen-
year-old Steve Harmon records his experiences in prison and in the
courtroom in the form of a film script as he tries to come to terms
with the course his life has taken.
    ISBN 0-06-028077-8. — ISBN 0-06-028078-6 (lib. bdg.).
    [1. Trials (Murder)—Fiction.   2. Prisons—Fiction.   3. Self-
perception—Fiction.   4. Afro-Americans—Fiction.]   I. Myers,
Christopher, ill. II. Title.
PZ7.M992Mon 1999   98-40958
[Fic]—dc21   CIP
                                                          AC

Typography by Alison Donalty
21 PC/LSCH 40 39
❖
First Edition

monster

The best time to cry is at night, when the lights are out and someone is being beaten up and SCREAMING for help. That way even if you sniffle a little they won't hear you. If anybody knows that you are crying, they'll start talking about it and soon it'll be your turn to get beat up when the lights go out.

There is a mirror over the steel sink in my cell. It's six inches high, and scratched with the names of some guys who were here before me. When I look into the small rectangle, I see a face looking back at me but I don't recognize it. It doesn't look like me. I couldn't have changed that much in a few months. I wonder if I will look like myself when the trial is over.

This morning at breakfast a guy got hit in the face with a tray. Somebody said some little thing and somebody else got mad. There was blood all over the place.

When the guards came over, they made us line up against the wall. The guy who was hit they made sit at the table while they waited for another guard to bring them rubber gloves. When the gloves came, the guards put them on, handcuffed the guy, and then took him to the dispensary. He was still bleeding pretty bad.

They say you get used to being in jail, but I don't see how. Every morning I wake up and I am surprised to be here.

If your life outside was real, then everything in here is just the opposite. We sleep with strangers, wake up with strangers, and go to the bathroom in front of strangers. They're strangers but they still find reasons to hurt each other.

Sometimes I feel like I have walked into the middle of a movie. It is a strange movie with no plot and no beginning. The movie is in black and white, and grainy. Sometimes the camera moves in so close that you can't tell what is going on and you just listen to the sounds and guess. I have seen movies of prisons but never one like this. This is not a movie

3

about bars and locked doors. It is about being alone when you are not really alone and about being scared all the time.

I think to get used to this I will have to give up what I think is real and take up something else. I wish I could make sense of it.

Maybe I could make my own movie. I could write it out and play it in my head. I could block out the scenes like we did in school. The film will be the story of my life. No, not my life, but of this experience. I'll write it down

in the notebook they let me keep.
I'll call it what the lady who is the
prosecutor called me.

MONSTER

Monster!

FADE IN: INTERIOR: Early morning in CELL BLOCK D, MANHATTAN DETENTION CENTER. Camera goes slowly down grim, gray corridor. There are sounds of inmates yelling from cell to cell; much of it is obscene. Most of the voices are clearly Black or Hispanic. Camera stops and slowly turns toward a cell.

INTERIOR: CELL. Sixteen-year-old STEVE HARMON is sitting on the edge of a metal cot, head in hands. He is thin, brown skinned. On the cot next to him are the suit and tie he is to wear to court for the start of his trial.

CUT TO: ERNIE, another prisoner, sitting on john, pants down.

CUT TO: SUNSET, another prisoner, pulling on T-shirt.

CUT TO: STEVE pulling blanket over his head as screen goes dark.

VOICE–OVER (VO)

Ain't no use putting the blanket over
your head, man. You can't cut this out;
this is reality. This is the real deal.

VO continues with anonymous PRISONER explaining how the Detention Center is the real thing. As he does, words appear on the screen, just like the opening credits of the movie *Star Wars*, rolling from the bottom of the screen and shrinking until they are a blur on the top of the screen before rolling off into space.

Monster!
The Story of
My
Miserable
Life

**Starring
Steve Harmon**

**Produced by
Steve Harmon**

**Directed by
Steve Harmon**

(Credits continue to roll.)

*The incredible story
of how* **one guy's life**
was **turned around**
by a **few events**
and how **he might**
spend **the rest of his life**
behind bars.
Told as it
**actually
happened!**

Written and directed by Steve Harmon
Featuring . . .

Sandra Petrocelli
as the Dedicated Prosecutor

Kathy O'Brien
as the Defense Attorney with Doubts

James King
as the Thug

Richard "Bobo" Evans
as the Rat

Osvaldo Cruz, member of the Diablos,
as the Tough Guy Wannabe

Lorelle Henry
as the Witness

José Delgado . . .
he found the body

And Starring
16-year-old Steve Harmon
as the Boy on Trial for Murder!

Filmed at the Manhattan Detention Center

Set design, handcuffs, and prison outfits by the State of New York

VO

Yo, Harmon, you gonna eat something? Come on and get your breakfast, man. I'll take your eggs if you don't want them. You want them?

STEVE (subdued)

I'm not hungry.

SUNSET

His trial starts today. He up for the big one. I know how that feels.

CUT TO: INTERIOR: CORRECTIONS DEPT. VAN. Through the bars at the rear of the van, we see people going about the business of their lives in downtown New York. There are men collecting garbage, a female traffic officer motioning for a taxi to make a turn, students on the way to school. Few people notice the van as it makes its way from the DETENTION CENTER to the COURTHOUSE.

CUT TO: PRISONERS, handcuffed, coming from back of van. STEVE is carrying a notebook. He is dressed in the suit and tie we saw on the cot. He is seen only briefly as he is herded through the heavy doors of the courthouse.

FADE OUT as last prisoner from the van enters rear of courthouse.

FADE IN: INTERIOR COURTHOUSE. We are in a small room used for prisoner-lawyer interviews. A guard sits at a desk behind STEVE.

KATHY O'BRIEN, STEVE's lawyer, is petite, red-haired, and freckled. She is all business as she talks to STEVE.

O'BRIEN

Let me make sure you understand what's going on. Both you and this King character are on trial for felony murder. Felony murder is as serious as it gets. Sandra Petrocelli is the prosecutor, and she's good. They're pushing for the death penalty, which is really bad. The jury might think they're doing you a big favor by giving you life in prison. So you'd better take this trial very, very seriously.

When you're in court, you sit there and you pay attention. You let the jury know that you think the case is as serious as they do. You don't turn and wave to any of your friends. It's all right to acknowledge your mother.

I have to go and talk to the judge. The trial will begin in a few minutes. Is there anything you want to ask me before it starts?

STEVE

You think we're going to win?

O'BRIEN (seriously)

It probably depends on what you mean by "win."

CUT TO: INTERIOR: HOLDING ROOM. We see STEVE sitting at one end of bench. Against the opposite wall, dressed in a sloppy-looking suit, is 23-year-old JAMES KING, the other man on trial. KING looks older than 23. He looks over at STEVE with a hard look and we see STEVE look away. Two GUARDS sit at a table away from the prisoners, who are handcuffed. The camera finds the GUARDS in a MEDIUM SHOT (MS). They have their breakfast in aluminum take-out trays that contain eggs, sausages, and potatoes. A Black female STENOGRAPHER pours coffee for herself and the GUARDS.

STENOGRAPHER

I hope this case lasts two weeks. I can sure use the money.

GUARD 1

Six days—maybe seven. It's a motion case. They go through the motions; then they lock them up.

(Turns and looks off camera toward STEVE.)

Ain't that right, bright eyes?

CUT TO: STEVE, who is seated on a low bench. He is handcuffed to a U-bolt put in the bench for that purpose. STEVE looks away from the GUARD.

CUT TO: DOOR. It opens, and COURT CLERK looks in.

14

COURT CLERK

Two minutes!

CUT TO: GUARDS, who hurriedly finish break-fast. STENOGRAPHER takes machine into COURTROOM. They unshackle STEVE and take him toward door.

CUT TO: STEVE is made to sit down at one table. At another table we see KING and two attorneys. STEVE sits alone. A guard stands behind him. There are one or two spectators in the court. Then four more enter.

CLOSE-UP (CU) of STEVE HARMON. The fear is evident on his face.

MS: People are getting ready for the trial to begin. KATHY O'BRIEN sits next to STEVE.

O'BRIEN

How are you doing?

STEVE

I'm scared.

O'BRIEN

Good; you should be. Anyway, just remember what we've been talking about. The judge is going to rule on a motion that King's lawyer made to suppress Cruz's testimony, and a few other things. Steve, let me tell you what my job is here. My job is to make sure the law works for you as well as against you, and to make you a human being in the eyes of the jury. Your job is to help me. Any questions you have, write them down and I'll try to answer them. What are you doing there?

STEVE

I'm writing this whole thing down as a movie.

O'BRIEN

Whatever. Make sure you pay attention. Close attention.

VO (COURT GUARD)

All rise.

The JUDGE enters and sits behind bench. He is tall and thin. He pushes his fingers through wisps of white hair and looks over the COURTROOM

16

before sitting. He is a 60-year-old New York judge and already looks bored with the case. The COURT GUARD signals for people to sit.

JUDGE

Prosecution ready?

SANDRA PETROCELLI, the prosecutor, stands. She is dressed in a gray business suit. She looks intense while still being attractive. Her hair and eyes are dark.

PETROCELLI

Ready, Your Honor.

JUDGE

Defense?

ASA BRIGGS, the lead counsel for the defense of JAMES KING, stands. He is dressed in a dark-blue suit and a light-blue tie. His eyes are also blue, and his hair is white.

BRIGGS

Ready.

O'BRIEN

Ready, Your Honor.

JUDGE

All right. I'm ruling the kid's testimony is admissible. You can bring up your motions relative to that ruling this afternoon or if there's a break. Hope everyone had a good Fourth of July?

BRIGGS

The usual barbecue and a softball game that reminded me that I can't run anymore.

O'BRIEN

With all the fireworks, it's my least favorite holiday.

JUDGE

Bring in the jury.

CUT TO: FILM WORKSHOP at Stuyvesant High School. A film on a small screen is just ending. It is a class project, and the camera is shaky. We watch as a girl on the screen walks slowly away.

Screen goes black, then dazzling white, then normal as lights go on.

We see MR. SAWICKI, film club mentor, and 9 STUDENTS, who are casually dressed.

SAWICKI

In a juried competition the ending would have hurt this piece, but otherwise it was interesting. Any comments?

We see STEVE raising his hand, looking much the same as he does in court.

STEVE

I liked the ending.

SAWICKI

I didn't say it was bad, but wasn't it predictable? You need to predict without predicting. You know what I mean? When you make a film, you leave an impression on the viewers, who serve as a kind of jury for your film. If you make your film predictable, they'll make up their minds about it long before it's over.

19

CUT TO: COURTROOM. We see the JURORS filing in and taking their seats.

STEVE (to attorney)

You think they look all right?

O'BRIEN

They are what we have for a jury. We have to deal with them.

CUT TO: LONG SHOT (LS) of PETROCELLI. She stands at the podium in front of the JURY. She smiles at the JURORS, and some smile back.

PETROCELLI

Good morning, ladies and gentlemen. My name is Sandra Petrocelli and I'm an Assistant District Attorney for the State of New York. I am representing the people in this matter, which you were informed during jury selection is a case of felony murder. We're here today basically because this is not a perfect world. The founding fathers of our country understood this. They knew that there would be times and circumstances during which our society would be threatened by the acts of individuals. This is one of those times. A citizen of our city, a citizen of our state and country, has been killed by people who attempted to rob him. To safeguard our society, a system of laws has been created. You, the jury, are part of this system of laws. I represent the State of New York and I am part of that system, as are the judge and all the participants in this trial. I will do my best to bring you the facts of this case, and I know you will do your best to judge the merits of the case.

Most people in our community are decent, hardworking citizens who pursue their own interests legally and without infringing on the rights of others. But there are also monsters in our communities—people who are willing to steal and to kill, people who disregard the rights of others.

On the 22nd of December of last year, at

approximately 4 o'clock in the afternoon, 2 men entered a drugstore on 145th
Street in Harlem. The State will contend that one of those men was Richard
"Bobo" Evans. The State will contend
that the other man who entered the
store at that time, and who participated in the robbery and the murder,
was James King.

PETROCELLI points to the table at which **JAMES KING** sits.

Mr. King is the man sitting at that
table who is wearing a brown suit and
is sitting at the right of the table.
You were introduced to him during the
jury selection process. He is one of the
men on trial here today. The purpose of
the 2 men entering the store on that
Monday was very simple. They were going
to rob the owner, 55-year-old Alguinaldo
Nesbitt. We will show that although the
2 men did not have a gun with them, the
owner of the store did have a gun for
which he had a license, and produced it
to defend his property.

Mr. Evans, who participated in the robbery, will testify that there was a struggle, which resulted in the gun being discharged and Mr. Nesbitt being killed. Mr. Nesbitt had every right to defend his property, every right not to be robbed. We all have that right.

Further, there will be evidence that prior to the robbery there was a plan, or conspiracy, to rob the store. Mr. Evans and Mr. King were to enter the store and do the actual robbery. Another of the planners of this crime was to stand outside the drugstore and impede anyone chasing the robbers. The young man who had this assignment will testify to his role in the affair. Yet another of the conspirators, the planners of this robbery that left a man dead, was to go into the store prior to the robbery to check it out, to make sure that there were no police in the store. To make sure that the coast was clear, as they say.

Two of the conspirators will testify to

their understanding of this fact. The man who was to enter the store and check it out is sitting at the other table. His name is Steven Harmon.

CUT TO: STEVE HARMON. Then: CU of the pad in front of him. He is writing the word *Monster* over and over again. A white hand (O'BRIEN's) takes the pencil from his hand and crosses out all the *Monster*s.

O'BRIEN (whispering)

You have to believe in yourself if we're going to convince a jury that you're innocent.

CUT TO: MS of PETROCELLI.

PETROCELLI

A medical examiner will testify to the cause of death, showing that the gunshot wound was fatal. Even though it was Mr. Nesbitt's gun, it was not Mr. Nesbitt who caused his own death. This was no suicide. This death was a direct result of the robbery. Very simply put, this is a case of murder. It is, more-over, a murder committed during a felonious act. The 2 defendants you see before you will be shown to be participants in that act and are being charged with felony murder. Later, the judge will give you instructions on how to consider the evidence presented. But there is no doubt in my mind, and I believe by the end of the trial there will be little doubt in yours, that these 2 men, James King and Steven Harmon, were all part of the robbery that caused the death of Alguinaldo Nesbitt. Thank you.

CUT TO: LS of COURTROOM. O'BRIEN is at attorneys' podium.

CUT TO: STEVE's MOTHER, on wooden bench in the gallery area, listening intently. Her face looks worried.

O'BRIEN

The State correctly says that the laws of a society provide protection for its citizens. When a crime is committed, it is the State that must apply the law in a manner that offers redress and that brings the guilty parties to justice. But the laws also protect the accused, and that is the wonder and beauty of the American system of justice. We don't drag people out of their beds in the middle of the night and lynch them. We don't torture people. We don't beat them. We apply the law equally to both sides. The law that protects society protects all of society. In this case we will show that the evidence that the State will produce is seriously flawed. We will show not only that there is room for reasonable doubt—and you will hear more about that idea at the end of this trial—but that the doubt that Steve Harmon has committed any crime, any crime at all, is overwhelming.

As Mr. Harmon's attorney all I ask of you, the jury, is that you look at Steve Harmon now and remember that at this moment the American system of justice demands that you consider him innocent. He is innocent until proven guilty. If you consider him innocent now, and by law you must, if you have not prejudged him, then I don't believe we will have a problem convincing you that nothing the State will produce will challenge that innocence. Thank you.

CUT TO: BRIGGS.

BRIGGS

Good morning, ladies and gentlemen. My name is Asa Briggs, and I will be defending Mr. King. Miss Petrocelli, representing the State, has presented this case in very broad and grandiose terms. But you will soon see that her key witnesses are among the most self-serving, heartless people imaginable. Some of them will begin their testimony by swearing that they are criminals. You will have the unpleasant task of listening to people who have committed crimes, who have lied and stolen, and in at least one instance has been an admitted, and let me emphasize this, an admitted accomplice to murder. But in

27

the end you will have the opportunity to judge the State's key witnesses and to deliver a just verdict. What I am asking you to do is just that. Judge what they bring up on the witness stand, and then deliver your just verdict. Thank you.

CUT TO: WITNESS STAND. JOSÉ DELGADO is on the stand. He is young, very well built, and articulate.

JOSÉ

I'm on until 9—the store closes at 9. So in the afternoon I either go home and grab a bite or go out for Chinese. That night I went out for Chinese. Usually I get something and eat it in the back. When I went out, everything was okay.

PETROCELLI

What time did you leave the drugstore?

JOSÉ

Four thirty, maybe 4:35 at the latest.

PETROCELLI

And what did you discover on your
return?

JOSÉ

At first I didn't see anything—which
I knew was weird because Mr. Nesbitt
wouldn't leave the place empty. I went
around behind the counter and I saw Mr.
Nesbitt on the floor—there was blood
everywhere—and the cash register was
open. A lot of cigarettes were missing,
too. Maybe 5 cartons.

PETROCELLI

And did you call the police?

JOSÉ

Yeah, but I knew Mr. Nesbitt was dead.

PETROCELLI

Mr. Delgado, are you familiar with the
so-called martial arts?

JOSÉ

That's my hobby. I have a black belt in
karate.

PETROCELLI

Is that fact pretty well known in the
neighborhood in which the drugstore
operated?

JOSÉ

Yeah, because whenever I was in a match
and it made the papers, Mr. Nesbitt
used to put the paper in the window.

PETROCELLI

Did police ever visit the drugstore?

JOSÉ

Sometimes they would come in and sneak
a smoke.

PETROCELLI

Nothing further.

BRIGGS

You state that 5 cartons of cigarettes
were missing?

JOSÉ

That's right.

BRIGGS

Five, not 6?

JOSÉ

Afterward I checked the inventory. It was 5.

BRIGGS

What medical school did you attend?

JOSÉ

None.

BRIGGS

But you said you knew that Mr. Nesbitt was dead. You were sure of it. That right?

JOSÉ

Pretty sure.

BRIGGS

Sure enough to stop and do inventory before trying to help your boss?

                    JOSÉ

I didn't take inventory right away, I
just noticed. You work in a store, you
notice if something is missing.

                    BRIGGS

How long did it take?

              JOSÉ (pissed)

I don't remember.

                    BRIGGS

Nothing further.

                  O'BRIEN

No questions.

       PETROCELLI (as JOSÉ steps down)

The state calls Salvatore Zinzi.

CUT TO: SAL ZINZI on the stand. He is nervous,
slightly overweight. He wears thick glasses, which
he touches over and over again as he testifies.

    32

PETROCELLI

Mr. Zinzi, where were you when you first became involved with this case?

ZINZI

Riker's Island.

PETROCELLI

Why were you there?

ZINZI

Stolen property. A guy sold me some baseball cards. They were stolen.

PETROCELLI

You knew they were stolen?

ZINZI

Yeah. I guess.

PETROCELLI

While you were at Riker's Island, did

you engage in a certain conversation with a Wendell Bolden?

ZINZI

Yes, ma'am.

PETROCELLI

You want to tell me about the conversation?

ZINZI

He said he knew about a drugstore holdup where a guy was killed, and he was thinking of turning the guy in to get a break.

PETROCELLI

And what did you do as a result of this conversation?

ZINZI

I called Detective Gluck and told him what I knew.

PETROCELLI

Because you wanted a break too. Is that right?

34

                    ZINZI

Yeah.

                 PETROCELLI

So Bolden told you he knew about the
crime. Was there anything else?

                    ZINZI

That was it.

                 PETROCELLI

Did he tell you about some cigarettes?

                    ZINZI

Yeah, he—

                   BRIGGS

Objection! She's leading.

                 PETROCELLI

Withdrawn. What else did he tell you?

                    ZINZI

That he got some cigarettes from this
guy. Two cartons.

PETROCELLI

Did he tell you the name of the person he got the cigarettes from?

ZINZI

No, just that he was sure the guy was involved in the holdup.

PETROCELLI

Nothing further.

CUT TO: BRIGGS at the podium.

BRIGGS

You wanted a break, Mr. Zinzi. Why did you need a break? You only had a few months to do; isn't that right?

ZINZI

Some guys were . . . sexually harassing me, sir.

BRIGGS

Sexually harassing? Were they calling you a sissy? What does "sexually ha-rass" mean to you?

36

ZINZI

They wanted to have sex with me.

BRIGGS

So to save yourself from being gang raped— Is that what they wanted to do to you?

ZINZI

Yeah.

BRIGGS

And you were afraid?

ZINZI

Yeah.

BRIGGS

You were afraid, and you would have said just about anything to get out of that situation. Isn't that right?

ZINZI

I guess so.

BRIGGS

Would you lie?

ZINZI

No.

BRIGGS

Let me get this straight, Mr. Zinzi.
You'd buy stolen goods for profit, rat
on somebody to save your own hide, but
you're too good to lie. Is that right?

ZINZI

I'm not lying now.

BRIGGS

As a matter of fact, this Bolden was
going to see what he could get out of
this, but you stole his chance, too.
Didn't you?

ZINZI

I guess.

BRIGGS

No further questions.

O'BRIEN

Mr. Zinzi, how long were you in jail?

ZINZI

Forty-three days.

O'BRIEN

Do people in jail look for stories to report to the police?

PETROCELLI (calmly)

Objection. The question's too vague.

O'BRIEN

Well, let me put it this way, Mr. Zinzi. This Mr. Bolden was going to use this story for his own benefit, is that right?

ZINZI

Right.

O'BRIEN

And you decided to use it for your benefit?

ZINZI

Right. Lots of guys in jail do that.

O'BRIEN

You use stories and you use people, right?

ZINZI

Sometimes.

O'BRIEN

And the outcome of your talking with the detective in question is that you were able to reach the District Attorney's office and strike a deal. Isn't that right? You were able to strike a deal that got you out of jail early? Isn't that right?

ZINZI

That's right.

O'BRIEN

You happy with the deal?

40

ZINZI

Yeah.

O'BRIEN

Nothing further.

PETROCELLI

Mr. Zinzi, do you know when you're lying
and when you're telling the truth?

ZINZI

Yes—sure.

PETROCELLI

You telling the truth now?

ZINZI

Yeah.

PETROCELLI

Nothing further.

FLASHBACK of 12-year-old STEVE walking in a
NEIGHBORHOOD PARK with his friend TONY.

TONY

They should let me pitch. I can throw straight as anything. (Scoops up a rock.) See the lamppost? (Throws rock. We see that it bounces in front of the post and careens slightly to one side.)

STEVE

You can't throw. (Picks up rock and throws it. We see it sail past the post and hit a YOUNG WOMAN. The TOUGH GUY she is walking with turns and sees the 2 young boys.)

TOUGH GUY

Hey, man. Who threw that rock? (He approaches.)

STEVE

Tony! Run!

TONY (taking a tentative step)

What? (TOUGH GUY punches TONY. TONY falls—TOUGH GUY stands over TONY as STEVE backs off. YOUNG WOMAN pulls TOUGH GUY away, and they leave.)

TONY and STEVE are left in the park with TONY
sitting on the ground.

TONY

I didn't throw that rock. You threw it.

STEVE

I didn't say you threw it. I just said
"Run." You should've run.

TONY

I'll get me an Uzi and blow his brains
out.

Notes:

I can hardly think about the movie, I hate this place so much. But if I didn't think of the movie I would go crazy. All they talk about in here is hurting people. If you look at somebody, they say, "What you looking at me for? I'll mess you up!" If you make a noise they don't like, they say they'll mess you up. One guy has a knife. It's not really a knife, but a blade glued onto a toothbrush handle.

I hate this place. I hate this place. I can't write it enough times to make it look the way I feel. I <u>hate</u>, <u>hate</u>, <u>hate</u> this place!!

CUT TO: INTERIOR: COURTROOM. WENDELL BOLDEN is on the stand. He is average height but heavily built with large, ashy hands. He acts like he's mad and wants everybody to know it.

PETROCELLI

Mr. Bolden, have you ever been arrested?

BOLDEN

Yeah. For B&E, and possession with intent.

PETROCELLI

Possession is obviously drugs and the intent to distribute. Can you tell the jury what B&E means?

BOLDEN

B&E. Breaking and entering.

PETROCELLI

And what were you in for when you spoke to Mr. Zinzi?

BOLDEN

Assault.

PETROCELLI

But the charges were dropped?

BOLDEN

Yeah, they were dropped.

PETROCELLI

Can you tell us about the conversation between you and Mr. Zinzi?

BOLDEN

I got some cigarettes from a guy who told me he was in on a drugstore robbery up on Malcolm X Boulevard. I knew a dude got killed, and I was thinking of trading what I knew for some slack.

PETROCELLI

As a matter of fact, didn't Mr. Zinzi also try to use that information himself?

BOLDEN

He called a detective he knew.

PETROCELLI

Can you name the person involved in the robbery?

BRIGGS

Objection! He can testify to the conversation—not the robbery, unless he was there.

PETROCELLI

Withdrawn. . . . So who gave you the information that he was involved in a robbery?

BOLDEN

Bobo Evans.

Camera pans to KING, who gives BOLDEN a dirty look.

CUT TO: EXTERIOR STOOP ON 141ST STREET. There is a small tricycle on the sidewalk. It is missing one wheel. The garbage cans at the curb are overflowing. Three young girls jump rope near the trash.

JAMES KING and STEVE are sitting on the steps.

49

A heavy woman, PEACHES, sits slightly above them, and a thin man, JOHNNY, stands. He is smoking a blunt.

KING (almost a drawl)

I need to get paid, man. I ain't got nothing between my butt and the ground but a rag.

STEVE

I hear that.

PEACHES

You can't even hardly make it these days. They talking about cutting welfare, cutting Social Security, and anything else that makes life a little easy. They might as well bring back slavery times if you ask me.

KING

If I had a crew, I could get paid. All you need is a crew with some heart and a nose for the cash.

PEACHES

Banks is where the money is.

JOHNNY

Naw. Bank money is too serious. The man comes down hard for bank money. You need to find a getover where nobody don't care—you know what I mean. You cop from somebody with a green card or an illegal and they don't even report it.

PEACHES

Restaurant owners got money, too. That's the only things left in our neighborhood—restaurants, liquor stores, and drugstores.

KING

What you got, youngblood?

STEVE

(Looks up at KING.) I don't know.

JOHNNY

Yo—what's your name? Steve. Since when you been down?

**CUT TO: INTERIOR: COURTROOM. BOLDEN is
still on the stand.**

BOLDEN

So he turned me on to 2 cartons for 5
dollars each. I asked him how he copped
and he said he was in a robbery in a
drugstore. I didn't say no more because
all I wanted was the smokes.

PETROCELLI

Did he tell you when the store was
robbed?

BOLDEN

He said it just went down.

PETROCELLI

And when did this conversation take
place?

BOLDEN

The day before Christmas. I remember
that because I gave a carton of cigarettes to my moms as a present.

PETROCELLI

No further questions.

BRIGGS

How well do you know Mr. Evans?

BOLDEN

I know him when I see him.

BRIGGS

Did you know him before Christmas?

BOLDEN

Not really.

BRIGGS

Let's see, now. You don't know this man, and yet when you ask him where he got the cigarettes, he's going to tell you that he got them from a holdup in which he was involved and in which a man was killed?

BOLDEN

If he wants to run his mouth, that's his business.

BRIGGS

And didn't you think it strange that a man would give out information that could be harmful to him if he had actually been involved in this case?

CUT TO: CU of JUROR looking bored.

CUT TO: CU of BOLDEN.

BOLDEN

Hey, I don't even care.

BRIGGS

Your assault charge was dropped—is that correct?

BOLDEN

Yeah.

BRIGGS

The maximum sentence for the assault was how long? Do you know?

BOLDEN

I wasn't convicted.

BRIGGS

Do you know the maximum sentence?

PETROCELLI

Objection.

JUDGE

Overruled; it's pertinent.

BRIGGS

So you saved yourself some heavy jail
time by pointing a finger at Mr. King,
isn't that right?

BOLDEN

I just wanted to do the right thing.
You know, like a good citizen.

BRIGGS (showing anger)

You were in jail trying to be a good
citizen? Or were you really just trying
to get out of jail and not caring who
you put in? Isn't that what you're
really doing? Well, isn't it?

PETROCELLI

Objection! Defense counsel is stepping over his bounds.

JUDGE

This is a good time for a break. I have some administrative tasks to get done this afternoon. Let's adjourn until tomorrow. I want to remind the jury not to discuss the case with anyone. We'll reconvene 9 A.M. tomorrow.

CUT TO: INTERIOR: DETENTION CENTER. It is night; the lights are out except for dim night-lights placed along the walls. We hear the sounds of fists methodically punching someone as the camera goes slowly down the corridor, almost seeming to look for the source of the hitting. We see two inmates silhouetted, beating a third. Another inmate is on lookout.

CUT TO: CU of STEVE lying on his cot. The sounds are in his cell, but he is not the one being beaten. We see the whites of his eyes, then we see him close his eyes as the sounds of the beating stop and the sounds become those of a sexual attack against the inmate who was beaten.

FADE OUT.

FADE IN: INTERIOR: STEVE's HOME. It is neatly furnished, clean. STEVE is watching TV with 11-year-old JERRY, his brother.

JERRY

You ever want to be a superhero? You know, save people and stuff?

STEVE

Sure. You know who I'd want to be? Superman. I'd be wearing glasses and stuff and people would be messing with me and then I'd kick butt.

JERRY

I bet you'd be a cool superhero. You know who you should be?

STEVE

Who?

JERRY

Batman. Then I could be Robin. (**STEVE** gives Jerry a brotherly shove.)

FADE OUT.

Wednesday, July 8

They take away your shoelaces and your belt so you can't kill yourself no matter how bad it is. I guess making you live is part of the punishment.

It's funny, but when I'm sitting in the courtroom, I don't feel like I'm involved in the case. It's like the lawyers and the judge and everybody are doing a job that involves me, but I don't have a role. It's only when I go back to the cells that I know I'm involved.

Miss O'Brien says that Petrocelli is using Bolden's testimony as part of a trail that will lead to me and James King. I think she is wrong. I think they are bringing out all of these people and letting them look terrible on the stand and sound terrible and then reminding the jury that they don't look any different from me and King.

I like the last scene in the movie, the one between me and Jerry. It makes me seem like a real person.

The man they called Sunset asked me if he could read the screenplay, and I let him. He liked it. Sunset said he liked

the name of the screenplay.
He said when he gets out, he
will have the word Monster
tattooed on his forehead.
I feel like I already have
it tattooed on mine.

   A preacher came to the
recreation room with a guard
this afternoon. He asked if anyone
wanted to talk with him or
share a moment of prayer. Two
guys said they did, and I was just
about ready to say I would
when Lynch, a guy who is going
on trial for killing his wife,
started cursing at the preacher
and saying that everybody
wanted to talk to him and act
like they were good when they

were just criminals. "It's too late to put up your holy front now," he said.

In a way he was right, at least about me. I want to look like a good person. I want to feel like I'm a **good** person because I believe I am. But being in here with these guys makes it hard to think about yourself as being different. We look about the same, and even though I'm younger than they are, it's hard not to notice that we are all pretty young. I see what Miss O'Brien meant when she said part of her job was to make

me look human in the eyes
of the jury.

When Lynch started cursing
at the preacher, the guards
took the preacher out, and then
they came back and turned
the television off and made us
go back to our cells.

Notes:
I couldn't sleep most of the
night after the dream. The
dream took place in the courtroom.
I was trying to ask questions
and nobody could hear me.
I was shouting and shouting but
everyone went about their business
as if I wasn't there. I hope
I didn't shout out in my sleep.

That would look weak to everybody. It's not good to be weak in here.

Every morning we get up and put on our court clothes. The talk is lawyer talk, with all the older guys talking about appeals and "mistakes" that the judge made.

I feel terrible. My stomach is gassy and bloated. I still can't go to the bathroom in front of everyone.

When we got in the court, there was a delay because the stenographer had brought the wrong power cord. The court officer was talking about termites.

FADE IN: COURTROOM. STEVE and KING are cuffed to a bench. COURT OFFICERS, PETROCELLI, STENOGRAPHER, JUDGE, BRIGGS, and O'BRIEN are present.

OFFICER 1

So this guy comes to the house and tells Vivian we got termites. I get home and she's all upset. I said no way we got termites. No way.

JUDGE

You ever see any termites?

OFFICER 1

What the heck's a termite look like?

O'BRIEN

Like an ant with wings.

OFFICER 1

Then I've never seen one.

OFFICER 2

I heard they hide in the wood.

JUDGE

What I don't understand is why they
have wings if they stay in the wood.

PETROCELLI

Are you going to let us do the affi-
davit on the crime scene?

JUDGE

Any objections?

BRIGGS

Who's going to read it in court?

JUDGE

The clerk.

BRIGGS

No objections.

O'BRIEN

What's with the detective?

PETROCELLI

He's having problems with a hemorrhoid
operation.

BRIGGS

Wait—I didn't know that—maybe we can keep him on the stand for an hour or 2.

CUT TO: CU of PETROCELLI.

PETROCELLI

Detective Karyl, can you describe the scene when you entered the drugstore?

CU: KARYL.

KARYL

It was pretty gruesome.

CUT TO: INTERIOR: Camera pans down aisles of neighborhood DRUGSTORE.

CUT TO: MS of JOSÉ DELGADO. He moves in slow motion. He is pale, glancing nervously at a point out of sight of camera. He is explaining something to DETECTIVE KARYL, who stands leaning against counter. The DETECTIVE is heavy, stooped.

CUT TO: A shot of open cash register.

CUT TO: COURTROOM.

PETROCELLI

Are these the pictures you took at that time?

KARYL

The crime-scene photographer took them.

O'BRIEN

May I see them?

MS: PETROCELLI hands pictures to O'BRIEN, who places them before her on desk.

CUT TO: CU of photos. We see legs of the slain drugstore owner, NESBITT.

CUT TO: BLACK-AND-WHITE SHOTS from various angles of body in grotesque position. Pictures flash in an increasingly contrasty and grainy format until they are hardly recognizable.

PETROCELLI

Detective Karyl, when you discovered the body, were there any signs of life in the victim?

KARYL

No. But I called the Emergency Medical Service, which is standard procedure.

PETROCELLI

And you noted the open cash register?

KARYL

That's correct. And at that time I asked the clerk was there anything else missing. Often in these cases you might find some cough medicine missing, or some attempt to open a restricted-drugs case. There's a market for drugs of any kind.

PETROCELLI

Did you look for other clues, and did you find any?

KARYL

We looked for other clues, but we didn't actually find anything.

PETROCELLI

Eventually you began questioning suspects in this case. How did you come across the suspects?

KARYL

We questioned a number of people we felt might have some knowledge of the crime. Then we received a tip from a person who claimed he knew what happened to the cigarettes.

PETROCELLI

That would be Mr. Zinzi?

KARYL

That's correct. He told us about Mr. Bolden. Then Mr. Bolden told us about Mr. Evans and Mr. King.

PETROCELLI

And both Zinzi and Bolden had their own motives in doing this?

KARYL

We often use information from informants, especially in murder cases.

PETROCELLI

And did you talk to Mr. King?

KARYL

To Mr. King and to some of his associates.

FADE OUT.

FADE IN: INTERIOR: 28TH PRECINCT. STEVE is sitting on a long, dark bench. He is dressed in cutoffs, sneakers, and a T-shirt. There is a basketball on the floor near him. DETECTIVE KARYL is sitting across from STEVE. He is eating a cheeseburger. Sometimes he talks with his mouth full. A Black detective, ARTHUR WILLIAMS, sits on the edge of the table. He is dressed much as STEVE is and looks only a few years older.

KARYL

They're saying that you pulled the trigger. King said the score was over but you turned back and shot Nesbitt. Why did you do that? I can't figure it.

STEVE

I don't know what you're talking about, man. I didn't do any stickup.

KARYL

You figured you didn't want to leave any witnesses, I guess.

WILLIAMS

What are we playing with this guy for? We don't need him. We got the case locked.

KARYL

The DA is thinking death penalty.

WILLIAMS

Death penalty? Chances are the judge will push for life without parole. And if they come clean, he might even go for 25 to life. You save a lot of time and money that way.

KARYL

I don't know. The victim was well respected in the neighborhood. Hard-working Black guy, worked his way up. He even sponsored a Little League team. The judge could go for the death penalty if they plead not guilty.

WILLIAMS

This guy's only 16. They won't kill him.

KARYL

What are you, a pessimist? Hope for the best.

CUT TO: Weird shot of INTERIOR: DEATH ROW. STEVE is seen walking down the hallway between two guards. He is brought into the death chamber. The guards are pale, almost greenish. They lay STEVE on the table for the lethal injection and strap him down.

CU of STEVE's face. He is terrified.

VO (as camera focuses on STEVE's face)

Open your legs; we have to plug up your butt so you don't mess yourself as you die.

STEVE's face grimaces with pain as they put in the plug.

CUT TO: INTERIOR: COURTROOM. KARYL is still on stand as BRIGGS cross-examines.

BRIGGS

Did you dust the area for fingerprints?

KARYL

It's my understanding that the crime-scene technicians didn't find any fingerprints they could establish as belonging to a perpetrator.

BRIGGS

Isn't it true that what you did in this case was to skip the investigation and run to your stoolies?

KARYL

We treat each case carefully. We don't just go through the motions.

BRIGGS

The cash register was handled, but you didn't find fingerprints, is that right?

KARYL

Not clear prints.

BRIGGS

How about the counter—was that dusted for fingerprints?

KARYL

Nothing clear enough to use.

BRIGGS

And it really isn't that hard to find people who are in jail or whom you arrest to swear that somebody else is a bad guy? Isn't that right?

KARYL

We check every story. We give everybody the benefit of the doubt.

BRIGGS

But you don't check fingerprints?

KARYL

We check them when we find them.

BRIGGS

Right. Nothing further.

CUT TO: INTERIOR: JAIL. An OLDER PRIS-
ONER sits on the john, his pants around his
ankles.

OLDER PRISONER

They got to give you some time. A guy
dies and you get time. That's the deal.
Why the hell should you walk? And don't
give me young. Young don't count when a
guy dies. Why should you walk?

STEVE

'Cause I'm a human being. I want a life
too! What's wrong with that?

OLDER PRISONER

Nothing. But there's rules you got to
follow. You do the crime, you do the
time. You act like garbage, they treat
you like garbage.

PRISONER 2

Yo, man. You acting like you a preacher or
something—but guess where you at? This
ain't no hotel.

OLDER PRISONER

But I ain't complaining.

PRISONER 2

But suppose he innocent?

OLDER PRISONER

You innocent?

STEVE

Yes.

OLDER PRISONER

Yeah, well, somebody got to do some time. They're going to lock somebody up.

PRISONER 3

How's he gonna say he's innocent? That's why they holding the trial—so the jury can say if he's innocent or not. What he says now don't even count.

OLDER PRISONER

Whatever. Anyone got a newspaper?

FADE OUT.

FADE IN: INTERIOR: WAITING ROOM. O'BRIEN enters and sits on bench with STEVE. STEVE's wrist is handcuffed to bench.

O'BRIEN (indicating cuffs)

This wasn't necessary.

STEVE

They just like to show they're in charge. How do you think the trial is going?

O'BRIEN

It could be going better.

STEVE (surprised)

What's wrong?

O'BRIEN

Well, frankly, nothing is happening that speaks to your being innocent. Half of those jurors, no matter what they said when we questioned them when we picked the jury, believed you were guilty the moment they laid eyes on you. You're young, you're Black, and you're on trial. What else do they need to know?

STEVE

I thought you're supposed to be innocent until you're proven guilty?

O'BRIEN

That's true, but in reality it depends on how the jury sees the case. If they see it as a contest between the defense and the prosecution as to who's lying, they'll vote for the prosecution. The prosecutor walks around looking very important. No one is accusing her of being a bad person. They're accusing you of being a monster. The jury can ask itself, Why should the prosecutor lie? Our job is to show that she's not lying, but she's simply made a mistake. How are you feeling? Is your stomach still upset?

STEVE

A little better.

O'BRIEN

This afternoon we have an important witness scheduled. This Osvaldo Cruz character. What do you know about him?

CUT TO: EXTERIOR: NEIGHBORHOOD STOOP. Fourteen-year-old OSVALDO CRUZ is slim, well built. He has a tattoo of a devil's head on his left forearm and a tattoo of a dagger on the back of his right hand between the thumb and forefinger. FREDDY ALOU, 16 and tough, sits fiddling with a beeper he is trying to repair. STEVE is sitting with them.

FREDDY (to STEVE)

What school you go to?

OSVALDO

He goes to that faggot school down-town. All they learn there is how to be a faggot.

FREDDY

You let him dis you like that, man?

OSVALDO

He don't have no choice. He mess with me and the Diablos will burn him up. Ain't that right, faggot?

STEVE

I can kick your narrow butt any day in the week.

OSVALDO

Well, here it is, so why don't you come and kick it?

FREDDY

You better chill; he hangs with some bad dudes.

OSVALDO

He don't hang with nobody. He's just a lame looking for a name. Ain't that right, Steve? Ain't that right?

STEVE

Why don't you shut up?

OSVALDO

You ain't got the heart to be nothing but a lame. Everybody knows that. You might be hanging out with some people, but when the deal goes down, you won't be around.

STEVE

Yeah, and you will be, huh?

CUT TO: INTERIOR: COURTROOM. OSVALDO is on the stand.

OSVALDO (softly, timidly)

So Bobo said to me if I didn't help him, he'd cut me up.

CUT TO: STEVE writing on pad.

CU: OSVALDO.

OSVALDO

He said he would cut me up and get my moms, too. I was, like, really scared of him.

PETROCELLI

Have you ever seen Bobo hurt anyone?

OSVALDO

I heard he messed up a dude in the projects.

BRIGGS

Objection.

JUDGE

Sustained.

PETROCELLI

Do you know as a matter of fact if Bobo
has hurt anyone in the hood?

BRIGGS

Objection! Unless the prosecutor is going to pass out glossaries to the jury,
I want her to use standard English.

JUDGE

Overruled.

OSVALDO

He told me he did some time for cutting
a guy in the projects.

PETROCELLI

Do you know how old Bobo is?

OSVALDO

Twenty-two.

PETROCELLI

And how old are you, Osvaldo?

BRIGGS

Objection! Why are we suddenly on a first-name basis?

PETROCELLI

And how old are you, Mr. Cruz?

OSVALDO

Fourteen.

PETROCELLI

You live on 144th Street; is that correct?

OSVALDO

Yeah, across from the school.

84

PETROCELLI

I'm going to give you a series of
names, and you will tell me if you know
any of them. James King?

OSVALDO

Yeah, that's him at that table in the
blue suit.

PETROCELLI

Let the record indicate that Mr. Cruz
has identified Mr. King. Steve Harmon?

OSVALDO

He's the Black guy sitting at the other
table.

PETROCELLI

Let the record show that Mr. Cruz has
identified Steve Harmon. (Turning back to
Osvaldo) All right. Did Mr. Evans, or
Bobo, make a proposition to you?

BRIGGS

Leading!

PETROCELLI

Your honor, Mr. Cruz is a juvenile!

BRIGGS

He's hostile? He's a juvenile. Do you mean to say he's hostile?

PETROCELLI

No, but you are.

JUDGE

That's not necessary, Miss Petrocelli. You haven't established Mr. Cruz as a hostile witness.

PETROCELLI

Mr. Cruz, how real did you think Mr. Evans's—Bobo's—threat was?

OSVALDO

I thought it was the real deal. You know, like I thought he would mess me up.

PETROCELLI

Were you afraid of Mr. King?

86

BRIGGS

Objection! If she wants to testify instead of the witness, fine. Swear her in,
but she can't lead the witness like that.

JUDGE

Sustained.

PETROCELLI

Did you participate in this robbery?

OSVALDO

Yes, I did.

PETROCELLI

Why?

OSVALDO

Because I was afraid of them. They were
all older than me.

PETROCELLI

Who exactly were you afraid of?

OSVALDO

Bobo, James King, and Steve Harmon.

PETROCELLI

And was Bobo the only one who actually threatened you?

BRIGGS

There she goes again!

JUDGE

Where's she going? That's not leading! You think that's leading? Look, I think it's a good time for a break, folks. Maybe we'll all be a bit more civil after a good night's sleep.

LS as JURY files out. Then the GUARDS come and cuff STEVE and JAMES KING. MS of OSVALDO passing STEVE. The two young men look at each other for a brief instant; then OSVALDO turns away.

FADE TO BLACK.

Thursday, July 9th

Miss O'Brien's saying that things looked bad for me was really discouraging. I wonder if the prosecutor knows what Osvaldo is really like. I wonder if she knows what I'm really like, or if she cares.

This morning one of the guys in the next cell expects a verdict. His name is Acie. He was telling everybody that he didn't care what they said about him. He held up a check-cashing place and shot the guard.

"All they can do is put me in jail," he said. "They can't touch my soul."

He said he needed the money and intended to pay it back once he got on his feet. He said that God understood and would give him another chance. Then he started crying.

His crying got to me. Miss O'Brien said the judge could sentence me to **25 years to life.** If he did, I would have to serve at least **21 years and 3 months.** I can't imagine being in jail for that long. I wanted to cry with the guy.

As I got dressed, I felt sick to my stomach. Mama leaves clean shirts and underwear for me.

I thought of her in the kitchen ironing the shirts. I think about myself so much, about what's going to happen to me and all, that I don't think about my folks that much. I know she loves me, but I wonder what she's thinking.

Mr. Nesbitt. I thought about Mr. Nesbitt and remembered the pictures they showed of him. When they were passing them to the jury I didn't look at them, but afterward, when the jury left, Miss O'Brien took them out and put them on the table in front of us. She made notes about them, but I could tell she wanted me to look at them. I looked at them.

91

Mr. Nesbitt's right foot was turned out. His left arm was lifted and bent at the elbow so that his fingers almost touched the side of his head. His eyes weren't completely closed.

Miss O'Brien looked at me— I didn't see her looking at me but I knew she was. She wanted to know who I was. Who was Steve Harmon? I wanted to open my shirt and tell her to look into my heart to see who I really was, who the real Steve Harmon was.

That was what I was thinking, about what was in

my heart and what that made me. I'm just not a bad person. I know that in my heart I am <u>not</u> a bad person.

Just before I had to go back to the cell block yesterday, I asked Miss O'Brien about herself. She said she was born in Queens, New York. She went to Bishop McDonnell High School, and then St. Joseph's College in Brooklyn. After that she worked her way through New York University Law School.

"And here I am," she said.

It sounded like a good life even though she said it like it was nothing special.

In the holding pen, across from where we enter the courtroom, the guards were talking about their lives. One wanted to talk about how much money his kid's teeth were costing to have them fixed. The other guard didn't have any kids and he wanted to talk about how the Yankees were doing.

We didn't start on time because one of the jurors was late.

"The little blonde," the guard who wasn't married said. "Her old man probably had something for her to do before she left the house."

They laughed. It must have
been funny.

While we were waiting, they
brought King in and handcuffed
him near me. I thought of the
movie, of what kind of camera
angle I would use.

I could smell the different
scents of him. He had on
aftershave lotion and some kind of
grease on his hair. I could separate
the smells. Please don't speak to
me, I prayed.

"They ain't got nothing yet," he
said. "Osvaldo don't mean nothing
'cause they let him walk. Anybody
can see that."

I didn't answer.

"You thinking about cutting a deal?" he asked.

King curled his lip and narrowed his eyes. What was he going to do, scare me? All of a sudden he looked funny. All the times I had looked at him and wanted to be tough like him, and now I saw him sitting in handcuffs and trying to scare me. How could he scare me? I go to bed every night terrified out of my mind. I have nightmares whenever I close my eyes. I am afraid to speak to these people in the jail with me. In the courtroom I am afraid of the judge. The guards terrify me.

I started laughing because it was funny. They do things to you in jail. You can't scare somebody with a look in here.

A court officer came in and got us. When I went into the courtroom, I saw a group of kids sitting in front. It looked like a junior high school class.

"Once the trial actually begins there will be no talking," the teacher with them said. "This is part of the American judicial system, and we have to respect every part of it."

When I looked at the kids in the class, they turned away from me quickly.

I sat down and looked straight ahead. It was easy to imagine myself sitting where they were sitting, looking at the back of the **prisoner.**

10 80 1- -17 -12 /59-4 8-23-/

W YORK STATE CORRECTION

10 80 1- -17 -12 /59-4 8-23-/

W YORK STATE CORRECTION

FADE IN: INTERIOR: COURTROOM. MS of JURORS. CU of a PRETTY BLACK JUROR. She is smiling.

CUT TO: CU of STEVE. He smiles.

CUT TO: CU of PRETTY BLACK JUROR. She stops smiling and looks quickly away.

MS of COURTROOM. STEVE has put his head down on the table. O'BRIEN pulls him up.

O'BRIEN

If you give up, they'll give up on you. (Then angrily) Get your head up!

STEVE lifts his head. There are tears on his face. As he wipes away the tears, we hear a VO of PETROCELLI as she continues with OSVALDO's testimony.

PETROCELLI

So what did Richard Evans, the man we are referring to as Bobo, suggest to you?

OSVALDO

He said he had a place all lined up. He said all I had to do was to slow anybody down who came out after them. I was going to push a garbage can in front of them.

CUT TO: PETROCELLI, who appears very confident. Then MS of front of COURTROOM.

PETROCELLI

When Bobo mentioned the other participants, did he specify what part they were to play in this robbery?

OSVALDO (getting tougher as he speaks)

He said that him and James King were going to go into the store and do the thing. Steve was going to be the lookout.

PETROCELLI

And how were the proceeds of this robbery going to be divided?

100

OSVALDO

Everybody was going to get a taste. I don't know how much exactly. But everybody was going to get a taste.

PETROCELLI

And is that taste, or share of the take, the reason you participated in this robbery?

OSVALDO

No, I was in because I was scared of Bobo.

PETROCELLI

Mr. Cruz, you're testifying against people you know. Are you testifying because you're getting a deal from the government?

OSVALDO

Yeah.

PETROCELLI

Nothing further.

MS of BRIGGS as he walks slowly to the podium. OSVALDO is obviously an important witness, and BRIGGS treats him like one.

                    BRIGGS

Mr. Cruz, when you were apprehended, did you make a statement to the police about your part in this crime?

                    OSVALDO

Yeah.

                    BRIGGS

You admitted to the police that you were a participant in this crime, isn't that true?

                    OSVALDO

A what?

                    BRIGGS

You were one of the people involved with the crime?

                    OSVALDO

Yeah, that's right.

BRIGGS

So for all practical purposes you were up to your neck in a crime in which a man was murdered. Is that right? Is that how you saw it?

OSVALDO

I guess so.

BRIGGS

And now that you're in trouble, you'd do pretty much anything to get out of trouble, wouldn't you? And when I say anything, I mean tell lies, get other people in trouble, anything?

OSVALDO

No.

BRIGGS

And when the Assistant District Attorney offered you a deal that would keep you out of jail, you jumped at it, didn't you?

OSVALDO

I wouldn't lie in court. I'm telling the truth.

BRIGGS

Well, I'm certainly glad you're telling the truth, Mr. Cruz. But let me ask you, Mr. Cruz, hasn't the prosecutor given you a choice? You go to jail or you put somebody else in jail? Isn't that your choice?

OSVALDO

I don't go around lying to people. Especially when I swear.

BRIGGS

And you did swear today, isn't that correct? And it wouldn't be right to lie under oath?

OSVALDO

Right.

BRIGGS

It wouldn't be right to lie under oath, but it would be just fine to go into a drugstore and stick it up? That's cool, isn't it?

OSVALDO

That was a mistake.

CU of BRIGGS's face showing absolute disgust.

BRIGGS

Nothing more.

O'BRIEN stands and takes her place at the podium.

O'BRIEN

Osvaldo, do you know how you were apprehended?

OSVALDO

I had a fight with my girlfriend and she called the police.

O'BRIEN

A fight? You mean an argument? A dis-agreement?

OSVALDO (quietly)

She found out I got another girl pregnant.

                    O'BRIEN

Are you a member of a gang?

                    OSVALDO

No.

                    O'BRIEN

So the information I have about you
belonging to a gang called the Diablos
is wrong?

A beat.

                    OSVALDO

No, that's right. I belong to the
Diablos.

                    O'BRIEN

So your first answer was a lie?

          OSVALDO (Looks toward Petrocelli.)

It was a mistake.

                    O'BRIEN

You also said that the robbery was a
mistake. Perhaps you can tell us the

106

difference between a mistake and a lie?

OSVALDO (ruffled)

Hey, I'm just trying to turn my life around. (Looks toward jury.) I made a mistake and now I figure it's about time I did the right thing.

O'BRIEN

How do you get into this gang, Mr. Cruz? Is there something you have to do to become a member?

OSVALDO (getting even tougher)

You have to fight a guy who's already in the club to show you got the heart.

O'BRIEN

And don't you have to do something else? Something involving a knife?

OSVALDO

You got to leave your mark on somebody.

O'BRIEN

Can you tell the jury exactly what it means to "leave your mark" on somebody?

OSVALDO

You have to cut them where it shows.

O'BRIEN

So to be a member of this gang, the Diablos, you have to fight a gang member and then cut someone. Usually that's done to a stranger, and the cut is made in the face, is that right?

OSVALDO

They don't do that anymore.

O'BRIEN

But Mr. Cruz, that's what you had to do, isn't it?

OSVALDO

Yeah.

O'BRIEN

But now you want us to believe that you

108

participated in this robbery because you were afraid of Bobo, and not because this is what you do?

OSVALDO

I was afraid.

O'BRIEN

Did you tell the Assistant District Attorney who questioned you that you were a member of the Diablos?

OSVALDO

Yeah, they knew.

O'BRIEN

You weren't afraid to fight a member of the Diablos to get into the gang. You weren't afraid of cutting a stranger in the face. You weren't afraid of beating up your girlfriend. But you were afraid of Bobo, is that right?

OSVALDO

Yeah.

CU of JUROR shaking her head.

DISSOLVE TO: INTERIOR: VISITORS' AREA of DETENTION CENTER. There is a table in the shape of a hexagon. One side leads to a tunnel through which the PRISONERS can enter. They sit on the inside while the VISITORS sit on the outside. We see STEVE sitting among the prisoners. He is wearing his orange prison garb. MR. HARMON, his father, sits on the outside of the table.

MR. HARMON

How are you doing?

STEVE

All right. You talk to Miss O'Brien?

MR. HARMON

She doesn't sound that positive. There's so much garbage going through that courtroom, she thinks that anybody in there is going to have a stink on him.

STEVE

She said she's going to put me on the stand. Give me a chance to tell my side of the story.

MR. HARMON

That's good. You need to tell them
that . . .

His voice fades away.

STEVE

I'm just going to tell them the truth,
that I didn't do anything wrong.

A beat as the father and son try to cope with the
tension.

STEVE

You believe that, don't you?

CU of MR. HARMON. There are tears in his eyes.
The pain in his face is very evident as he struggles
with his emotions.

MR. HARMON

When you were first born, I would lie
up in the bed thinking about scenes of
your life. You playing football. You
going off to college. I used to think
of you going to Morehouse and doing the

same things I did when I was there. I never made the football team, but I thought—I dreamed you would. I even thought about getting mad at you for staying out too late—there you were lying on the bed in those disposable diapers—I wanted the real diapers but your mother insisted on the kind you didn't have to wash, just throw away. I never thought of seeing you—you know—seeing you in a place like this. It just never came to me that you'd ever be in any kind of trouble. . . .

MS: STEVE and MR. HARMON. An incredibly difficult moment passes between them. STEVE searches his father's face, looking for the reassurance he has always seen there.

STEVE

How's Mom doing?

MR. HARMON

She's struggling. It's hard on all of us. I know it's hard on you.

STEVE

I'll be okay.

STEVE puts his head down and begins to weep. MR. HARMON turns away, then reaches back and touches STEVE's hand. A GUARD crosses quickly and moves the father's hand away from his son.

MR. HARMON (choking with emotion)

Steve. It's going to be all right, son. It's going to be all right. You're going to be home again and it's going to be all right.

The scene blurs and darkens. There is the sound of STEVE's FATHER sobbing.

Notes:

I've never seen my father cry
before. He wasn't crying like
I thought a man would cry.
Everything was just pouring out of
him and I hated to see his face.
What did I do? What did I <u>do?</u>
Anybody can walk into a drugstore
and look around. Is that what I'm
on trial for? I didn't do nothing!
I didn't do nothing! But everybody
is just messed up with the pain.
I didn't fight with Mr. Nesbitt.
I didn't take any money from him.
Seeing my dad cry like that was
just so terrible. What was going on

between us, me being his son and him being my dad, is pushed down and something else is moving up in its place. It's like a man looking down to see his son and seeing a monster instead.

Miss O'Brien said things were going bad for us because she was afraid that the jury wouldn't see a difference between me and all the bad guys taking the stand. I think my dad thinks the same thing.

Contra Costa County Library
Clayton
11/17/2022 4:00:44 PM

- Patron Receipt -
- Charges -

ID: 21901027451685

item: 31901066733454
Title: Monster /
Call Number: YA FIC MYERS, W.
Due Date: 12/8/2022

All Contra Costa County Libraries will
be closed on Thursday, November 24th
and will close by 6 pm on Wednesday,
November 23rd. In addition,
Prewett Library will also be closed
on Friday, Nov 25th. Items may be
renewed online at http://ccclib.org
or by calling 1-800-984-4636, menu
option 1. Book drops will be open
for returns.

FADE IN: EXTERIOR: STEVE's NEIGHBOR-
HOOD. Camera pans. Homeless men have built a
cardboard "village" on rooftops. Then: to edge of
roof, where we see a crowd in the street below. As
camera zooms in, we pick up a cacophony of
sounds. Gradually one sound becomes clearer.
The accent is West Indian, and a ground-level camera comes up on two dark, somewhat heavy and
middle-aged WOMEN.

WOMAN 1

I think it's a shame, a terrible shame.

WOMAN 2

What happened?

CUT TO: STEVE; he is holding a basketball and is
within earshot of the 2 women.

WOMAN 1

They stuck up the drugstore and shot
the poor man.

WOMAN 2

Oh, these guns! Is he all right?

117

WOMAN 1

Miss Trevor say he dead. They had 2 ambulances.

WOMAN 2

Two people got shot?

WOMAN 1

I don't think 2 people got shot, but 2
ambulances came. One came from Harlem
Hospital.

WOMAN 2

It's probably those crack people. They
say they'll do anything for that stuff.

WOMAN 1

Was he married? I didn't see no woman
working in the store.

WOMAN 2

That young Spanish boy? I don't think
he married.

WOMAN 1

No, girl, he ain't the owner. The old

man owned that place. I think he from
St. Kitts.

WOMAN 2

Oh, you know it's a shame. You know it
is.

**LS: STEVE makes his way through crowd. He
does not have the basketball. He is walking, then
trots as the camera pulls back. He is running as
camera looks from high angle, and we can no
longer distinguish STEVE. We hear VO of women
as above.**

WOMAN 1

I'd move away from here, but there's
no place to go. I wouldn't live in
California.

WOMAN 2

California is a lot worse than Harlem.

WOMAN 1

But they say the weather is nice.

**Camera pans down the street, past playing kids
and stores to a basketball that lies in the gutter.**

CUT TO: Television news; the shot is grainy, the reception poor as if it is in the home of a ghetto resident.

VO (NEWSCASTER)

In New York's Harlem, yet another holdup has ended in a grisly scene of murder. Alguinaldo Nesbitt, a native of St. Kitts, was found shot and killed in his drugstore.

CUT TO: Television shot of front of drugstore. Small children are gathered around trying to get a peek inside.

CU: NEWSCASTER. He is a handsome, light-skinned Black who speaks with a precise television-newscaster accent.

NEWSCASTER

Late yesterday afternoon 2 armed and masked bandits rushed into this neighborhood drugstore behind me. They first demanded money and, when the store owner, 55-year-old Alguinaldo Nesbitt was slow in handing over the money, viciously ended his life. Residents of the neighborhood are in absolute dismay. (To NEIGHBORHOOD RESIDENT) Sir, can you tell me just how shocked you are by this tragedy?

CUT TO: NEIGHBORHOOD RESIDENT.

NEIGHBORHOOD RESIDENT

I ain't shocked. People getting killed and everything and it ain't right but I ain't shocked none. They killed a little girl just about 2 months ago and she was just sitting on her stoop.

CUT TO: STEVE's APARTMENT. We see him sitting and watching the news program. We see his brother pick up the remote and change the program. We watch 30 seconds of a *Road Runner* cartoon.

CUT TO: CU of STEVE. He is staring straight ahead, mouth open, in absolute shock as the reflected colors from the cartoon move across his face.

DISSOLVE TO: TWO WEEKS LATER; INTERIOR: STEVE's KITCHEN. Door opens. MRS. HARMON enters with a bag of groceries. She puts it down.

MRS. HARMON

Mrs. Lucas said they got those guys that killed the drugstore owner. (She turns on the television.) You have anything to eat?

STEVE

I had some cereal. See if you can find the news. You think it's on the news?

MRS. HARMON is putting away the groceries when an image of the front of the drugstore appears on the screen. She sits down, obviously pleased that the culprits have been caught.

FEMALE NEWSCASTER

An arrest has been made in the robbery and murder in an uptown drugstore. The police announced today the arrest of Richard Evans, known in the community as Bobo. Mayor Rudy Giuliani says that he is determined to stop crime in all areas of the city.

CUT TO: PRESS CONFERENCE with MAYOR GIULIANI and POLICE BRASS.

MAYOR GIULIANI

The idea that we're just trying to stop crime in white or middle-class areas is nonsense. Everyone living in the city deserves the same protection.

CUT TO: EXTERIOR: MS of a sullen BOBO handcuffed and being led to police van. He glowers at camera. Prisoner he is handcuffed to winks at camera.

CUT TO: INTERIOR: STEVE's BEDROOM. He is lying on his bed, eyes open but not seeing anything. We hear first the doorbell ring and then his mother calling him, but he doesn't react.

CUT TO: MRS. HARMON, who wipes her hands on a towel and heads toward door. She stops and looks through peephole. CU on her face. There is a worried look as she opens the door.

MRS. HARMON

(Calls to him.) Steven?

STEVE

Yeah? (He comes out and sees DETECTIVES WILLIAMS and KARYL.)

WILLIAMS

We need you to come down to the pre-cinct with us. Just a few questions.

STEVE

Me? About what?

WILLIAMS

Some clown said you were involved with that drugstore stickup just before Christmas. You know the one I mean?

STEVE

Yeah, but what do I have to do with it?

WILLIAMS (as they handcuff Steve)

You know Bobo Evans?

MRS. HARMON (mildly panicked)

Why are you handcuffing my son if you just want to ask him a few questions? I don't understand.

WILLIAMS

Ma'am, it's just routine. Don't worry
about it.

MRS. HARMON

What do you mean don't worry about it,
when you're handcuffing my son? (There is
panic in her eyes as she looks at STEVE, who
looks away.) What do you mean don't worry
about it? I'm coming with you! You're
not just snatching my son off like he's
some kind of criminal. Wait till I get
my coat. Just wait a minute! Just wait
a minute!

CUT TO: JERRY standing in doorway, holding
comics. He looks from MOTHER to STEVE. He
reaches out toward his brother as the detectives
hustle the handcuffed teenager out the door.

CUT TO: MS of STEVE sitting in back of patrol
car.

CUT TO: Two OLD MEN in front of John-John's
Bar-B-Q looking at the scene as the car drives off.

CUT TO: LS of block engaged in normal activity.

THEN: MRS. HARMON rushes from house, looks desperately around, and moves quickly down the street. She gets almost to the corner, then stops, realizing she doesn't know where STEVE is being taken.

Friday, July 10th

   Miss O'Brien was mad today. She
said that Petrocelli was using a
cheap trick. The judge said he
was calling a half-day session
because he needed to hear pleas
in another case. O'Brien said that
Petrocelli wanted to leave as
bad an image in the mind of the
jury as she could. She brought up
the photographs again and made
sure that the jury saw them a
second time. Miss O'Brien said she
wanted the jurors to take the bad
images home with them over the
weekend and live with them.
   The photos were bad, real bad.
I didn't want to think about them

or know about them. I didn't look at the jury members when they were looking at the pictures.

I thought about writing about what happened in the drugstore, but I'd rather not have it in my mind. The pictures of Mr. Nesbitt scare me. I think about him lying there knowing he was going to die. I wonder if it hurt much. I can see me at that moment, just when Mr. Nesbitt knew he was going to die, walking down the street trying to make my mind a blank screen.

When I got back to the cell and changed my clothes, I had to mop the corridors with four other guys. We were all dressed in the orange jumpsuits they give you and the guards made us line up. The water was hot and soapy and had a strong smell of some kind of disinfectant. The mops were heavy and it was hot and I didn't like doing it. Then I realized that the five guys doing the mopping must have all looked alike and I suddenly felt as if I couldn't breathe. I tried to suck the air into my lungs, but all I got was the odor of the disinfectant and I started gagging.

"You vomit—you just got more to clean up!" the guard said.

I held it in and kept swinging the big mop across the floor. To my right and left the other prisoners were doing the same thing. On the floor there were big arcs of gray, dirty water and swirls of stinking, brown bubbles. I wanted to be away from this place so bad, away from this place, away from this place.

I remembered Miss O'Brien saying that it was her job to make me different in the eyes of the jury, different from Bobo and Osvaldo and King. It was me, I thought as I tried not to throw up, that had wanted to be tough like them.

FADE IN: Four-way SPLIT-SCREEN MONTAGE:
Three images alternate between shots of witnesses
and defendants. We hear only 1 witness at a time,
but the others are clearly still talking on other
screens. In upper left screen is DETECTIVE
WILLIAMS. Lower left is ALLEN FORBES, a City
Clerk. Lower right is DR. JAMES MOODY, Medical
Examiner. The upper right screen is sometimes
black, sometimes a stark and startling white.
Occasionally the images of those not speaking are
replaced with images of KING or STEVE, and we
get REACTION SHOTS.

FORBES

It was a registered gun. Our records
show that Mr. Nesbitt applied for a
license to have a gun on the premises
in August of 1989. That permit was
still in effect. The gun was licensed
to him from that time.

VO (PETROCELLI)

So there was nothing unusual or illegal
about the gun being in the drugstore?
Is that correct, Mr. Forbes?

FORBES

Presumably he wanted it for the store. That is correct.

SWITCH TO: DETECTIVE WILLIAMS.

WILLIAMS

I arrived at the crime scene at 5:15. There was some merchandise on the floor of the drugstore in between the counters. The body of the victim was lying halfway . . . his legs were half sticking out from behind the counter. I looked around the counter and observed a middle-aged Black male of approximately 200 pounds. It was pretty clear that he was dead. There was an emergency medical crew there, and they were just packing it in when I arrived. I looked around the scene and saw the gun. A uniformed patrolman pointed it out to me. I didn't know at the time if it was the gun that killed the victim or not. There wasn't any way to tell without tests.

The cash register was open. The change was still in there, but no bills. Also, there were several cartons of cigarettes on the floor, and the clerk mentioned that several cartons of cigarettes were missing. We chalked the body, then had it turned.

VO (PETROCELLI)

What do you mean when you say you chalked the body?

WILLIAMS

That's when you put a chalk mark around the perimeter of the body to show the position you found it in. We had photos taken, then we chalked the body so we could turn it over and see if there was any possible evidence beneath the victim. I didn't see anything there. From the money being gone from the register, I figured it was a stickup and homicide. The guys from the Medical Examiner's office wanted to move the body. It was time for them to get off, and I allowed them to take it.

VO (PETROCELLI)

Detective Williams, during the course of your investigation of the crime did you have occasion to speak to a Mr. Zinzi?

WILLIAMS

My partner got a call from this guy on Riker's Island. That was Sal Zinzi. He was doing 6 months on a stolen property charge. There were a few guys in there who were giving him a hard time. He wanted out pretty bad. He told me about a guy who had told him about a guy who was selling cigarettes. It was a slim lead, but we followed it up until we found a Richard Evans.

VO (PETROCELLI)

Known on the street as Bobo?

WILLIAMS

Known on the street as Bobo, right. We picked him up and he admitted involvement in the stickup.

SWITCH TO: DR. MOODY.

MOODY (Nods constantly as he testifies.)

The bullet entered the body on the left side and traversed upward through the lung. It produced a tearing of the lung and heavy internal bleeding and also went through the esophagus. That also produced internal bleeding. The bullet finally lodged in the upper trapezius area.

VO (PETROCELLI)

And were you able to recover the bullet from that area?

MOODY

Yes, we were.

VO (PETROCELLI)

Dr. Moody, can you tell with reasonable certainty the time and cause of death?

MOODY

Death was caused by a combination of trauma to the internal organs, which put the victim into a state of shock, as well as by the lungs filling with blood.

135

He wouldn't have been able to breathe.

VO (PETROCELLI)

You mean he literally drowned in his own blood?

REACTION SHOT: STEVE catches his breath sharply.

REACTION SHOT: KING has head tilted to one side, seemingly without a care.

Saturday, July 11th

Before she left, Miss O'Brien
warned me not to write anything in
my notebook that I did not want
the prosecutor to see.

I asked Miss O'Brien what she
was going to do over the weekend,
and she gave me a really funny
look, and then she told me she was
probably going to watch her niece
in a Little League game.

"I'm sorry," she said. "I didn't
mean to cut you off."

She smiled at me, and I felt
embarrassed that a smile should
mean so much. We talked awhile
longer and I realized that I did not
want her to go. When I asked her

137

how many times she had appeared in court, her mouth tightened and she said, "Too many times."

She thinks I am guilty. I know she thinks I am guilty. I can feel it when we sit together on the bench they have assigned for us. She writes down what is being said, and what is being said about me, and she adds it all up to guilty.

"I'm not guilty," I said to her.

"You should have said, 'I didn't do it,'" she said.

"I didn't do it," I said.

Sunset got his verdict yesterday. Guilty.

"Man, my life is right here," he said. "Right here in jail. I know I did

the crime and I _got_ to do the time.
It ain't no big thing. It ain't no big
thing. Most they can give me is
7 to 10, which means I walk in
5 and a half. I can do that without
even thinking on it, man."

It's growing. First I was scared
of being hit or raped. That being
scared was like a little ball in the
pit of my stomach. Now that ball is
growing when I think about what
kind of time I can get. Felony
murder is 25 years to life. My
whole life will be gone. A guy said
that 25 means you have to serve
at least 20. I can't stay in
prison for 20 years. I just can't!

Everybody in here either talks

about sex or hurting somebody or what they're in here for. That's all they think about and that's what's on my mind, too. What did I do? I walked into a drugstore to look for some mints, and then I walked out. What was wrong with that? I didn't kill Mr. Nesbitt.

Sunset said he committed the crime. Isn't that what being guilty is all about? You actually do something? You pick up a gun and you aim it across a small space and pull a trigger? You grab the purse and run screaming down the street? Maybe, even, you buy some baseball cards that you know were stolen?

The guys in the cell played

140

dirty hearts in the afternoon
and talked, as usual, about their
cases. They weighed the evidence
against them and for them and
commented on each other's cases.
Some of them sound like lawyers.
The guards brought in a guy
named Ernie who was caught
sticking up a jewelry store. Ernie
was small, white, and either Cuban
or Italian. I couldn't tell. The police
had caught him in the act. He
had taken the money and the
jewelry and then locked the two
employees in the back room with a
padlock they used on the front
gates.

"But then I couldn't get out
because they had a buzzer to

open the front door," Ernie said. "I didn't know where the buzzer was and I had locked the two dudes who knew up in the back."

He waited for two hours while people came and tried to get into the store before he called the police. He said he wasn't guilty because he hadn't taken anything out of the store. He didn't even have a gun, just his hand in his pocket like he had a gun.

"What they charging you with?" somebody asked.

"Armed robbery, unlawful detention, possession of a deadly weapon, assault, and menacing."

But he felt he wasn't guilty. He had made a mistake in going into the store, but when the robbery didn't go down there was nothing he could do.

"Say you going to rob a guy and he's sitting down," Ernie went on. "You say to him, 'Give me all your money,' and then he stands up and he's like, seven feet tall, and you got to run. They can't charge you with robbing the dude, right?"

He was trying to convince himself that he wasn't guilty.

There was a fight just before lunch and a guy was stabbed in the eye. The guy who was stabbed was screaming, but that didn't

stop the other guy from hitting him
more. Violence in here is always
happening or just about ready
to happen. I think these guys like
it—they want it to be normal
because that's what they're used
to dealing with.

If I got out after 20 years, I'd be
36. Maybe I wouldn't live that long.
Maybe I would think about killing
myself so I wouldn't have to live that
long in here.

Mama came to see me. It's her
first time and she tried to explain
to me why she hadn't been here
before, but she didn't have to.
All you had to see were the tears

running down her face and the whole story was there. I wanted to show strong for her, to let her know that she didn't have to cry for me.

The visitors' room was crowded, noisy. We tried to speak softly, to create a kind of privacy with our voices, but we couldn't hear each other even though we were only 18 inches away from each other, which is the width of the table in the visitors' room. I asked her how Jerry was doing and she said he was doing all right. She was going to bring him tomorrow and I could see him from the window.

"Do you think I should have got a

Black lawyer?" she asked. "Some of the people in the neighborhood said I should have contacted a Black lawyer."

I shook my head. It wasn't a matter of race.

She brought me a Bible. The guards had searched it. I wanted to ask if they had found anything in it. Salvation. Grace, maybe. Compassion. She had marked off a passage for me and asked me to read it out loud: "'The Lord is my strength and my shield; my heart trusted in him, and I am helped: therefore my heart greatly rejoiceth; and with my song will I praise him.'"

"It seems like you've been in here so long," she said.

"Some guys have done a whole calendar in here," I said.

She looked at me, puzzled, and then asked what that meant. When I told her that doing a calendar meant spending a year in jail, she turned her head slightly and then turned back to me. The smile that came to her lips was one she wrenched from someplace deep inside of her.

"No matter what anybody says . . ." She reached across the table to put her hand on mine and then pulled it back, thinking a guard might see her. "No matter what anybody says, I know you're innocent, and I love you very much."

And the conversation was over. She cried. Silently. Her body shook with the sobs.

When she left I could hardly make it back to the cell area. "No matter what anybody says . . ."

I lay down across my cot. I could still feel Mama's pain. And I knew she felt that I didn't do anything wrong. It was me who wasn't sure. It was me who lay on the cot wondering if I was fooling myself.

CUT TO: EXTERIOR: MS of MARCUS GARVEY PARK in HARLEM. STEVE is sitting on a bench, and JAMES KING sits with him. KING is bleary-eyed and smokes a joint as he talks.

KING

Yeah, well, you know, I found where the payday is. You know what I mean?

STEVE

Yeah, I guess.

KING

You guess? What you guessing about when I'm so flat I ain't got enough money to buy a can of beer? I need to put together a payroll crew. Get my pockets fat. F-A-T. I talked to Bobo and he's down, but Bobo liable not to show. When he shows, he shows correct but sometime he act like a spaceman or something.

STEVE

Bobo's not Einstein.

KING

Whatever. You don't have to be no Einstein to get paid. All you got to have is the heart. You got the heart?

STEVE

For what?

KING

To get paid. I got a sure getover. You know that drugstore got burned out that time? They got it all fixed up now. Drugstores always keep some money.

STEVE

That's what Bobo said?

KING

Yeah. All we need is a lookout. You know, check the place out—make sure ain't no badges copping some z's in the back. You down for it?

CUT TO: CU of STEVE looking away.

CUT TO: CU of KING.

150

KING

So, what it is?

This phrase is repeated as the camera moves farther and farther away, growing louder and louder
as STEVE and KING become tiny figures in the
bustling mosaic of Harlem.

Sunday, July 12th

They had scrambled eggs,
potatoes, and corned beef hash
for breakfast. A lot of guys don't
go to breakfast on Sunday, and
the ones that do can just about
eat as much as they want. The
guy behind the steam table put a
lot of food on my plate and gave
me a smile. In here you don't smile
back at people who smile at you,
so I just walked away.

They had church services and
I went. There were only 9 guys in
the service, and 2 of them got
into a fight. It was a vicious fight
and the minister called the

guards. They came in and started saying things like "Break it up" and "Okay, back off." But they said it in this calm voice as if nothing was really going on and they didn't care if the two guys were fighting or not.

We got locked down because of the fight and we were told we had to stay in our cells until 1 o'clock. One o'clock is when the visiting hours start on Sundays.

In the cell we played bid whist and another fight almost started when one of the guys thought somebody had dissed him.

I think I finally understand why there are so many fights. In here all you have going for you is the little surface stuff, how people look at you and what they say. And if that's all you have, then you have to protect that. Maybe that's right.

When we got out, most of the guys drifted into the recreation area, and somebody put the television on. There was a baseball game on but it didn't look real. It was guys in uniforms playing games on a deep green field. They were playing baseball as if baseball was important and as if all the world wasn't in jail, watching them from a completely different world. The world I came from, where I had my family around me and friends and kids I went to school with and even teachers, seemed so far away.

I looked down in the street from the corridor leading to the recreation room. Downtown New York was almost empty on Sundays. The thousands of people who streamed through the streets on weekdays were away in their homes. I was looking for Jerry. They didn't allow kids in the visiting area, which was funny.

It was funny because if I wasn't locked up, I wouldn't be allowed to come into the visiting room.

At a quarter past one, some women were down in the streets calling up to other women. Then I saw my parents and Jerry.

Jerry was tiny in the street, standing on the corner. The window was screened and I knew he couldn't see me, but I raised my hand anyway and waved to him. I wanted to tell Jerry that I loved him. I also wanted to tell him that my heart was not greatly rejoicing, and I was not singing praises.

My parents came, one at a time, and they were both upbeat and full of news about the neighborhood and about Jerry.

"Did you see him down in the street?" Mama asked.

I told her yes and tried to smile with her. Her eyes were smiling but her voice cracked. In a way I think

she was mourning me as if I were
dead.

They left and there was still too much Sunday left in my life.

I looked over the movie again. I need it more and more. The movie is more real in so many ways than the life I am leading. No, that's not true. I just desperately wish this was only a movie.

Monday is the State's case. This is what Miss O'Brien said. Monday they bring out their star witnesses.

FADE IN: INTERIOR: COURTROOM. There is a feeling of expectation in the air. PETROCELLI, BRIGGS, and O'BRIEN are talking to the JUDGE. PETROCELLI makes a joke and O'BRIEN laughs briefly. They return to their respective tables and the JUDGE nods to the COURT STENOG-RAPHER, who straightens up, ready to take down the day's proceedings.

PETROCELLI

The State calls Lorelle Henry.

Camera swings to the rear of the COURTROOM. An Assistant District Attorney ushers in LORELLE HENRY. The diminutive 58-year-old retired school librarian is neatly dressed. She was once a beautiful woman and is still quite attractive, looking far younger than her stated age. She moves with grace to the witness stand, avoiding looking at either the jury or the defendants.

PETROCELLI

Mrs. Henry, do you remember an incident that occurred last December in Harlem?

161

HENRY

Yes, I do.

PETROCELLI

Can you tell us about that incident?

HENRY

My granddaughter had a cold. It was just a few days before Christmas and I didn't want it to ruin her Christmas. I had taken her to Harlem Hospital and they said it wasn't serious, but she was still coughing. I went into the drugstore to look for some cough medicine. I was looking over the medicines, trying to figure out which would be best for her, when I heard someone arguing.

PETROCELLI

Do you know what the argument was about?

HENRY

No, I don't.

162

PETROCELLI

Then what happened?

HENRY

The store owner, Mr. Nesbitt, came over
to see what the argument was about, and
I heard one of the men who was involved
in the argument say to him—ask him
where the money was.

PETROCELLI

How sure are you that this is what he
said?

HENRY (nervously)

Not that sure. It's what I think I
heard.

PETROCELLI

And what did you see during this time?

HENRY

I saw two young men engaged in an argument. Then I saw one of them grab the
drugstore owner by the collar. (She grabs
her own collar to demonstrate.)

163

PETROCELLI

And then what did you do?

HENRY

And then I left the store as quickly as I could. I thought there might be trouble.

PETROCELLI

Mrs. Henry, do you recognize anyone present today in this courtroom who was also in the drugstore on the day to which you are referring?

HENRY

The gentleman sitting at that table was one of the men arguing. (She points to KING.)

PETROCELLI

Let the record show that Mrs. Henry has indicated that the defendant, James King, was one of the men she saw in the drugstore on that day. Mrs. Henry, do you remember the day you witnessed the incident at the drugstore?

HENRY

The 22nd of December. It was a Monday. I didn't want Tracy—that's my grand-daughter—missing too much school. I thought if she could get through the next day or so, she would be all right because of the Christmas break.

PETROCELLI

Thank you. Nothing further.

CUT TO: BRIGGS at podium.

BRIGGS

Mrs. Henry, did you have occasion to see some photographs of Mr. King?

HENRY

Yes, I did. At the police station.

BRIGGS

You heard about the robbery and the death of Mr. Nesbitt and you went to the police; is that correct?

HENRY

That's correct.

BRIGGS

And the police showed you a series of pictures—would you say a thousand pictures?

HENRY

A thousand? No, maybe 30 to 40.

BRIGGS

Maybe 20?

HENRY

I think more than 20.

BRIGGS

Would you say 27?

HENRY

I couldn't say for sure.

BRIGGS

So the truth is that the police showed you a few photographs and asked you to

cooperate with them in finding a killer.
Is that correct?

HENRY

More or less.

BRIGGS

More or less? Well, I want to get to the truth of this matter, Mrs. Henry. The police did show you the pictures, and they were looking for your cooperation in finding a killer? Is that correct?

HENRY

Yes.

BRIGGS

Mrs. Henry, while you were looking over the pictures, were there moments of hesitation? Were there moments when you weren't quite sure, or did you recognize Mr. King as soon as you saw his picture?

HENRY

I didn't recognize him at first, but then I did—the pictures look different than he does in person.

BRIGGS

So how did you recognize him if he looks different in person than he does in the photographs?

HENRY

I finally recognized him. And when I see him now, I recognize him.

BRIGGS

Mrs. Henry, were you ever given a description of Mr. King? Ever told how much he weighed or how tall he was?

HENRY

No, I was not.

BRIGGS

You said that someone said something about Mr. Nesbitt showing them where the money was, is that correct?

HENRY

That's correct.

BRIGGS

Do you remember who said that? Was it the man you think was Mr. King?

HENRY

I don't know.

BRIGGS

You testified in a pretrial hearing that you had some trouble testifying that Mr. King was involved in this event, is that correct?

HENRY

I have trouble testifying against a Black man, if that's what you mean.

BRIGGS

But somehow you don't have trouble identifying Mr. King at this time; isn't that so?

HENRY

I think I'm doing the right thing. I think I'm identifying the right man.

BRIGGS

Did you ever identify Mr. King in a lineup?

HENRY

Yes, I did.

BRIGGS

Was that before or after you saw the photographs?

HENRY

That was after I saw the photographs.

BRIGGS

And how many men were in the lineup?

HENRY

I believe there were 6.

BRIGGS

Six. Only 6. Nothing further.

CUT TO: O'BRIEN sitting at the table. She looks up toward the judge and shakes her head.

O'BRIEN

No questions, Your Honor.

CUT TO: PETROCELLI.

PETROCELLI

Is there any question in your mind that the man you identified from photographs is the same man who sits at this table?

HENRY

No, there is not.

PETROCELLI

Thank you. Nothing further.

MS of BRIGGS, his ASSOCIATE, and JAMES KING.

BRIGGS (to KING)

When this guy gets on the stand, I want you to take notes. Just write down any questions you want us to ask him.

KING

Like what?

171

BRIGGS

Don't worry about it. We just need the jury to know we're challenging this guy.

PETROCELLI

Richard "Bobo" Evans, your honor.

Camera pans to side of COURTROOM, where a COURT OFFICER opens the door and leans out. He holds the door open until RICHARD "BOBO" EVANS enters. He is a big man, heavy, and ugly. His hair is uncombed, and his orange prison jumpsuit is wrinkled.

BRIGGS

Your honor, could we have a sidebar?

BRIGGS, O'BRIEN, PETROCELLI and COURT STENOGRAPHER go to side of JUDGE's bench, where they speak in whispers.

BRIGGS

Why is he dressed in a prison uniform? The prosecution is going to try to connect him to my client. With him in prison gear, that prejudices my client.

172

PETROCELLI

He refused to put on a suit. We made the offer.

BRIGGS

It's still prejudicial.

JUDGE

To tell you the truth, I don't think it's going to make that much of a difference. This guy looks like a basket case and he's going to act like one. I don't want to hold the case up while you convince this guy to wear a suit. Let's get on with the case.

BRIGGS

I'd like to establish the objection.

JUDGE

Okay, and I'll overrule it. Let's get going.

They return to their respective previous positions with **PETROCELLI** at the podium.

PETROCELLI

Please state your full name.

BOBO

Richard Evans.

PETROCELLI

Mr. Evans, how old are you?

BOBO

Twenty-two.

PETROCELLI

And are you sometimes known by another
name? A nickname or tag?

BOBO

They call me Bobo.

PETROCELLI

Now, Mr. Evans, do you know the people
who are seated at these two tables, Mr.
Steven Harmon and Mr. James King?

BOBO

Yeah, I know them.

174

PETROCELLI

How long have you known them?

BOBO

I been knowing King all my life. I just met the other guy before the robbery went down.

PETROCELLI

Before we go any further, Mr. Evans, I notice that you are wearing a prison uniform. What is your current status?

BOBO

I'm doing a heavy and a half up at Greenhaven.

PETROCELLI

Will you explain to the jury what a heavy and a half is?

BOBO

Seven and a half to 10 years.

PETROCELLI

And what are you doing the time for?

BOBO

Selling drugs.

PETROCELLI

And you've been arrested before?

BOBO

I been arrested for (Hesitates.) . . .
breaking and entering, grand theft
auto, and one time for taking a car
radio and one time for fighting a guy
what died.

PETROCELLI

So the arrest for fighting a guy that
died was manslaughter, is that right?

BOBO

Yeah. I got three years.

PETROCELLI

I think the record will show you got
5 to 10 years and served 3. Is that
correct?

BOBO

Whatever.

PETROCELLI

Mr. Evans, can you tell me what happened on the 22nd of December of last year?

BOBO

Me and King planned out a getover and we done it.

PETROCELLI

Can you explain to the jury what this particular "getover" was.

BOBO

We hit a drugstore.

PETROCELLI

Can you tell me as much as you can about the plan and about what actually happened?

BOBO

We went over to the place and sat down on a car outside. Then we got the sign from him—

PETROCELLI

Let the record show that Mr. Evans is pointing toward Mr. Harmon. Go on.

O'BRIEN

Objection!

JUDGE

Sustained. Is he identifying him or not?

PETROCELLI

Can you identify the man from whom you got the sign that everything was all right?

BOBO

That's him, sitting next to the woman with the red hair.

PETROCELLI

Let the record show that Mr. Evans is identifying Mr. Harmon. Go on.

BOBO

So we got the sign that everything was

cool. King took a hit on some crank we had and then we went in. We started a beef with the dude behind the counter. He came up with a chrome and started shouting and stuff.

PETROCELLI

A chrome?

BOBO

Yeah. A gun. Anyway, King was trying to get the gun from him and I was going for the money. Then I heard the gun go off. I looked over and saw the guy falling down and King was holding the chrome. We grabbed what we wanted and split. That was it.

PETROCELLI

What else did you grab besides the money?

BOBO

We took some cigarettes and left.

PETROCELLI

Then what did you do?

BOBO

Then we went down to that chicken joint over Lenox Avenue, across from the bridge. We got some fried chicken and some wedgies and some sodas.

PETROCELLI

Who was with you at this time?

BOBO

Just me and King.

PETROCELLI

When did you find out that Mr. Nesbitt, the drugstore owner, was dead?

BOBO

The word was in the street that night.

PETROCELLI

What happened to the money you got from the robbery?

BOBO

Like I said, we spent some of it on

fried chicken and wedgies. Then me and King split the rest.

PETROCELLI

You indicated that Mr. Harmon gave you the all-clear signal so you could proceed with the robbery, is that right?

BOBO

Yeah.

PETROCELLI

And was he to get part of the money?

O'BRIEN

Objection! If Miss Petrocelli wants to testify in—

JUDGE

Sustained! Sustained! Let's not get carried away. Rephrase the question.

PETROCELLI

Was anybody else to share in the money?

181

BOBO

The little Puerto Rican boy was supposed to get a taste and King's friend
was supposed to get a taste.

PETROCELLI

You said that you received a sign from
Mr. Harmon. Can you tell me what that
sign was?

BOBO

He was supposed to tell us if there was
anybody in the drugstore. He didn't say
nothing so we figured it was all right.

PETROCELLI

And you definitely saw Mr. Harmon coming from the drugstore, as planned?

BOBO

Right.

PETROCELLI

As far as you know, was the shooting of
Mr. Nesbitt accidental?

BOBO

I asked King what happened, and he said he had to light him up because he was trying to muscle him. He was an old man, but he was strong like some of them old West Indian brothers. You know what I mean?

PETROCELLI

Can you tell me how it was that you were arrested?

BOBO (embarrassed)

I sold the cigarettes to this guy—his name is Bolden, Golden—something like that. Then he sold some to a white boy and then the white boy dropped a dime on him and he dropped it on me. Once it got going it was 4-1-1, 9-1-1, 7-1-1, I guess they was dropping dimes with 800 numbers, too. Then the cops came and started talking to me. I said I didn't know nothing about it, but then I got busted on a humble and went down.

PETROCELLI

Can you explain to the jury how you were busted?

BOBO

Man, this lame-looking brother with an attaché case come up to me and said he wanted to cop some rocks. I was so knocked out by this bourgie dude asking for crack that I slept the real deal. I laid the rocks on him and he slapped the cuffs on me. Cops don't usually show lame. That was definitely not correct.

JUDGE

He carried an attaché case?

BOBO

Can you believe that crap?

PETROCELLI

Mr. Evans, you were promised a deal for your testimony. Can you tell us what that deal is?

184

BOBO

If I tell what happened, the truth, then I can cop a plea to a lesser charge and pull 10 to 15.

PETROCELLI

Are you telling the truth today?

BOBO

Yeah.

PETROCELLI

Nothing further.

CUT TO: ASA BRIGGS. He shuffles through some papers, nods approvingly, and then approaches the podium from which he will question BOBO.

BRIGGS

Mr. Evans, you admit that you were in the drugstore, is that correct?

BOBO

Yeah.

BRIGGS

You also admit that you were in the drugstore to commit a felony. Is that correct?

BOBO

Yeah.

BRIGGS

So you were in the drugstore, committing a felony—the felony in this case being robbery—and during the commission of that felony a man was killed?

BOBO

Yeah.

BRIGGS

So by your own admission, under New York State law you are guilty of felony murder, for which the possible penalty is 25 years to life without parole?

BOBO

So?

BRIGGS

And you haven't been tried for this crime yet. So if you ever want to walk the streets again, you had better find somebody to take the weight. Isn't that correct?

BOBO

What you saying? Am I trying to cop a plea? I just told you I was trying to cop.

BRIGGS

And we know who you are, don't we? You're the dope dealer and the thief who could see a man killed and then go over to a fast-food place and have a nice meal. That's who you are, right?

BOBO

I didn't have nothing to eat all day.

BRIGGS

So after you killed Mr. Nesbitt—

BOBO

I didn't kill him.

BRIGGS

As far as this jury knows, you are the only man who admits being in the drug-store when Mr. Nesbitt was killed. You admitted to planning the robbery. You also admitted to taking the cigarettes, and you admitted to being there when Mr. Nesbitt was lying on the floor of the store he had worked so hard for. But now you blame somebody else for the killing to get a break for yourself, isn't that right?

BOBO

I think King was high or he wouldn't have shot the dude. He didn't have to shoot him. He's the cause of me being in this mess.

BRIGGS

Not you? You didn't want to do the stickup?

BOBO

Man, later for you.

BRIGGS

Nothing further.

JUDGE

Miss O'Brien?

O'BRIEN (from her chair)

Mr. Evans, when did you have a conversation with Mr. Harmon about this robbery?

PETROCELLI (smiling)

Perhaps counsel wants to approach the podium?

O'BRIEN stands and goes slowly to the podium, looking at her notes.

BOBO

I didn't have a conversation with him. He's King's friend.

O'BRIEN

So let me get this straight. What was

Mr. Harmon supposed to do if there were cops in the drugstore?

BOBO

Give us a signal.

O'BRIEN

And what was that signal to be?

BOBO

Something to let us know there were cops in there.

O'BRIEN

And if there were no cops in there, what was he supposed to do?

BOBO

I don't know.

O'BRIEN

You said you planned the robbery with Mr. King. Didn't he tell you?

BOBO

I thought King had it hooked up. He

told me he had everything straight.

O'BRIEN

You testified that you did not have a gun when you entered the drugstore. Is that correct?

BOBO

Right.

O'BRIEN

How did you know—how do you know now—that the gun that was used was not brought into the drugstore by whoever it was you were with?

BOBO

King said he didn't have no gun.

O'BRIEN

So you're relying pretty much on what you've been told about this robbery. Is that correct?

BOBO

'Cept what I seen.

O'BRIEN

And what you saw was when you were actually involved in the holdup?

BOBO

That's right.

O'BRIEN

Did you ever talk to Osvaldo?

BOBO

I said a few words to him.

O'BRIEN

You told him that he had better participate in the crime or you would hurt him?

BOBO

He wanted in.

O'BRIEN

But he testified that the only reason he was involved in this stickup was that he was afraid of you.

BOBO

I wouldn't bring anybody into a serious jam unless they wanted to be there. You can't rely on nobody that don't want to be there.

O'BRIEN

When you were in the drugstore—and you have admitted being there—did you see anyone else in the store?

BOBO

I didn't see the lady.

O'BRIEN

But you know now that a lady was in the store. Is that correct?

BOBO

Yeah.

O'BRIEN

How did you find that out, from Mr. King?

BOBO

Detective told me.

O'BRIEN

King told you about the plans, or what he wanted you to know of them. The police told you about the witness. Are you sure you were there?

BOBO

I told you I was there.

O'BRIEN

As a matter of fact, your deal depends on your admitting you were there, doesn't it, Mr. Evans?

BOBO

Yeah.

O'BRIEN

Did you talk to Osvaldo after the stickup?

BOBO

No.

194

O'BRIEN

Did you talk to Mr. Harmon?

BOBO

No.

O'BRIEN

How about the money? Weren't you supposed to split the money up?

BOBO

When we found out the guy was dead, we
decided to lay low.

O'BRIEN

Who is the "we" who decided to lay low?

BOBO

Me and King.

O'BRIEN

Thank you; nothing further.

CUT TO: PETROCELLI, adjusting her glasses.

PETROCELLI

Prior to the robbery, just before the robbery, what were you and Mr. King doing?

BOBO

Just before we went in?

PETROCELLI

Yes, just before you went in, what were you doing?

BOBO

Waiting for him to come out.

PETROCELLI

Who are you referring to when you say "him"?

BOBO

Him, that guy sitting over there.

PETROCELLI

Let the record show that Mr. Evans is referring to Steve Harmon. Nothing further.

O'BRIEN

(Stands quickly.) But you had not spoken to
Mr. Harmon prior to the stickup?

BOBO

Naw.

O'BRIEN

And you didn't speak to him after the
stickup or split any money with him?

BOBO

I told you we decided to lay low. We
would have given him his cut later when
things cooled down.

O'BRIEN

Did that time ever come?

BOBO

I don't know what King did.

O'BRIEN

But as far as you know, there was no
money given to Mr. Harmon.

BOBO

I don't know what King done.

O'BRIEN

Nothing further.

CUT TO: MS of JURORS from STEVE's point of view (POV). One JUROR, a middle-aged man, looks directly toward the camera for a long time. The camera then moves away as if STEVE has turned away from the accusing stare.

PETROCELLI

The people rest.

FADE OUT.

FADE IN: Concentric colorful circles and hurdy-gurdy music: A hustling, bustling CARTOON CITY comes alive on the screen. Then a small CARTOON MAN, dressed in an old-fashioned nightgown, looks out of his window.

CARTOON MAN (shouting)

The people rest!

On-screen all CARTOON CHARACTERS stop, cars screech to a stop, and then everybody sleeps. The people are resting.

CUT TO: INTERIOR: COURTROOM.

JUDGE

I'll take motions this afternoon after lunch. The defense can start its case the first thing in the morning. It's a nice day out, and we'll adjourn and give the jury the rest of the day off unless somebody has an objection.

We see the JURY leave, then the various parties leave in turn. We see MRS. HARMON come over and talk to O'BRIEN. STEVE's MOTHER is disturbed as a COURT OFFICER comes over and stands near STEVE.

FADE OUT.

Miss O'Brien came to see me this afternoon. She looked tired. She said that Bobo's testimony hurt us a lot and that she had to find a way to separate me from King, but King's lawyer wanted to make sure the jury connected us because I looked like a pretty decent guy. She talked to me for almost an hour. Several times she patted me on the hand. I asked her if that meant that she thought we were going to lose the case. She said no, but I don't believe her.

I am so scared. My heart is beating like crazy and I am having trouble breathing. The trouble I'm in keeps looking bigger and bigger. I'm overwhelmed by it. It's crushing me.

It is a nice day on the outside. On the street below, people walk in what looks like a crisscross pattern across the narrow streets. There are yellow cabs inching along. On the corner there is a cart that sells food, frankfurters or sausages I guess, and sodas. People stand around buying what they want, then move away. It looks like something I would like to do, move away from where I am.

Tomorrow we start our case, and I don't see what we are going to do. I hear myself thinking like all the other prisoners here, trying to convince myself that everything will be all right, that the jury can't find me guilty because of this reason or that reason. We lie to ourselves here. Maybe we are here because we lie to ourselves.

Lying on my cot, I think of everything that has happened over the last year. There was nothing extraordinary in my life. No bolt of lightning came out of the sky. I didn't say a magic word and turn into somebody different. But here I am, maybe on the verge of losing my life, or the life I used to have. I can understand why they take your shoelaces and belt from you when you're in jail.

Miss O'Brien made me write down all the people in my life who I love and who love me. Then I had to write down the people who I admire. I wrote down Mr. Sawicki's name twice.

Mr. Briggs will present King's defense first. Miss O'Brien will go second, but she says she has to be careful because if she says anything that makes King look bad and Mr. Briggs attacks her, it will look bad for me.

"We can use some friends," she said.

When she left and I had to go back to the cell area, I was more depressed than I have been since I've been here. I wish Jerry were here. Not in jail, but somehow with me. What would I say to him? Think about all the tomorrows of your life. Yes, that's what I would say. Think about all the tomorrows of your life.

When the lights went out, I think I heard someone crying in the darkness.

FADE IN: INTERIOR: COURTROOM: DOROTHY MOORE is on the stand. She is a brown-skinned, fairly pleasant-looking woman. She looks sincerely at ASA BRIGGS.

BRIGGS

And what time do you remember Mr. King coming to your home that afternoon?

MOORE

Three thirty.

BRIGGS

And you're sure of the time?

MOORE (confidently)

I am quite sure, sir.

BRIGGS

Nothing more.

PETROCELLI

Mrs. Moore, how often does Mr. King come to your house?

MOORE

About twice a month. He's my cousin.

PETROCELLI

Do you remember the purpose of the visit?

MOORE

He was just dropping by. He saw a lamp that he thought I might like and he brought it by. We talked about Christmas coming up.

PETROCELLI

He bought the lamp for you?

MOORE

Yes, he did.

PETROCELLI

Do you remember if he was working at the time? Did he have a job?

MOORE

I don't think so.

PETROCELLI

And still he took his money to buy you a lamp. You remember how much the lamp cost?

MOORE

No, I don't.

PETROCELLI

But that was nice of him, wasn't it?

MOORE (subdued)

I think it was.

PETROCELLI

And you like him a lot, don't you?

MOORE

I wouldn't lie for him, if that's what you're saying.

PETROCELLI

Before this visit, when did you last see Mr. King?

MOORE

I guess a few weeks before that. I
don't know the exact date.

PETROCELLI

What kind of work was he looking for?

MOORE

Just a job. I don't know.

PETROCELLI

Does he have a driver's license?

MOORE

I don't know.

PETROCELLI

You really don't know a lot about your
cousin, do you?

MOORE

I know I saw him that day.

PETROCELLI (condescendingly)

And what do you do for a living?

MOORE

I do day's work, but I wasn't working that week, because I had hurt my ankle. I went to the doctor that Monday, and you can check that.

PETROCELLI

You don't have to verify what you were doing, Mrs. Moore. Did anybody see Mr. King at your home on that day?

MOORE

I don't think so.

PETROCELLI

Do you still have the lamp? The lamp Mr. King so kindly bought for you?

MOORE

It broke.

PETROCELLI

Should I take that to mean you no longer have the lamp?

MOORE

They don't make things to last anymore. I think it was made in Korea or someplace like that.

PETROCELLI

Again, should I take that to mean that you no longer have the lamp?

MOORE

I don't have it now, but I did have it.

PETROCELLI

Yes, of course. Thank you. Nothing further.

CUT TO: GEORGE NIPPING on stand. He is about 50 and wears wire-rimmed glasses. He speaks precisely and generally makes a good impresssion.

BRIGGS

Mr. Nipping, do you know, as a matter of fact, if Mr. King is right-handed or left-handed?

NIPPING

He's left-handed. I know that because when he was a kid, I went out and bought him a glove, a baseball glove, and I had to take it back because he was left-handed.

BRIGGS

Have you ever known him to do anything of significance with his right hand?

NIPPING

No, I've never seen him use his right hand for anything.

We see STEVE writing on a pad.

CUT TO: The pad. O'BRIEN is writing a note under STEVE's question, which reads "What's that about?" She writes: "The wound was on the left side of the body, which might mean that the shooter was right-handed. It's a weak argument."

BRIGGS

And for the record, how long have you known Mr. King?

NIPPING

I'd say about 17 to 18 years.

BRIGGS

Thank you.

CUT TO: NIPPING on stand facing PETROCELLI.

PETROCELLI

Have you ever seen Mr. King shoot a man?

NIPPING

No, I haven't.

PETROCELLI

So when he shoots a gun, you don't know what hand he uses. Is that right?

BRIGGS

Objection!

PETROCELLI (ignoring objection)

If Mr. King was struggling with someone and the gun happened to be on the right side, do you know what he would do?

NIPPING

No, I don't.

PETROCELLI

Nothing further.

CUT TO: FILM CLASS. MS of MR. SAWICKI.

SAWICKI

There are a lot of things you can do with film, but you don't have an unlimited access to your audience. In other words, keep it simple. You tell the story; you don't look for the camera technician to tell the story for you. When you see a filmmaker getting too fancy, you can bet he's worried either about his story or about his ability to tell it.

CUT TO: INTERIOR: ROOM where lawyers meet with their clients. SPLIT SCREEN: One side is O'BRIEN, pacing nervously. On the other side is STEVE, sitting.

214

O'BRIEN

You're going to have to take the stand—
look at the jury and let the jury look
at you—and say that you're innocent. I
know the judge will tell the jury not
to infer anything if you don't take the
stand, but I believe that the jury
wants to hear from you. I think they
want to hear your side of the story.
Can you handle it?

We see STEVE nodding in the affirmative.

O'BRIEN

The prosecutor's strongest point against
you is the connection between you and
King. She has Bobo admitting to being in
on the robbery and his link to King.
You've told me you know King. I don't
know why you've chosen this man as an
acquaintance, but it's going to hurt you
big-time if you don't manage to get some
distance between you and him in the eyes
of the jury. You're going to have to
break the link. He's sitting there looking surly. Maybe he thinks he's tough;

I don't know. I do know you'd better put some distance between yourself and whatever being a tough guy represents.

You need to present yourself as someone the jurors can believe in. Briggs isn't going to put King on the stand. That helps you, but when he sees us separating you from him, he's going to realize that his client is in trouble.

STEVE

How do you know he won't testify?

O'BRIEN

King made a statement to the police when he was arrested. He said he didn't know Bobo. But the prosecution can prove that's a lie. So if he takes the stand, they can use his own statements against him and he's cooked. If you don't testify, you'll just make the tie between you and King stronger in the mind of the jury. I think you have to testify. And the way you spend the rest of your youth might well depend on how much the jury believes you.

STEVE

That woman said that King was with her.

O'BRIEN

Right, but Petrocelli didn't even bother with a lengthy cross-examination. Did you notice that? She dismissed Mrs. Moore with her tone of voice. A cousin who likes him testifes that he was with her. Big deal. Against all the evidence against him, it doesn't count for very much. His lawyer is going to rely on his closing argument to win the case, and I don't think that's going to be effective unless he's very, very lucky. Cases are won on closing arguments only on television, not in a real courtroom.

SINGLE MS: We see STEVE nodding, but he is looking down. We see O'BRIEN looking at him, studying him closely. She sits down and takes a deep breath.

O'BRIEN

(Puts a paper cup on the table.) Okay, Steve, now stay with me. We're going to play a little game. I'm going to take this cup and place it on the table. Then I'm going to ask you some questions. When I like the answers you give me, I'll leave the cup facing up. When I don't like the answers, I'll turn it upside down. You figure out what's wrong with the answer you gave me. All right?

STEVE

Why? (O'BRIEN doesn't answer. Then we see STEVE nod his assent.)

O'BRIEN

Did you know James King?

STEVE

No?

CUT TO: O'BRIEN turns the cup down.

STEVE

Yeah, casually.

CUT TO: O'BRIEN turns the cup up.

O'BRIEN

When was the last time you spoke to him
before the robbery?

STEVE

Last summer?

CUT TO: O'BRIEN turns the cup down.

STEVE

I don't know for sure. I mean, he's not
like a guy I talk with a lot.

CUT TO: O'BRIEN turns the cup up.

THEN: The camera moves farther and farther
away from the pair. We see another prisoner and
lawyer enter the room. We don't hear O'BRIEN's
questions or STEVE's answers but we see
O'BRIEN turning the cup.

FADE TO BLACK.

FADE IN: INTERIOR: CELL at nighttime: We
barely see the outlines of the inmates, 2 of whom
are sleeping on the floor.

VO (INMATE 1)

The prosecutor said I was lying. I wanted to ask her what she expected me to do when telling the truth was going to get me 10 years.

VO (INMATE 2)

When they got you in the system, it ain't time to get all holy. You in the system, you needs to get out the system.

VO (INMATE 1)

What's the truth? Anybody in here knows what the truth is? I don't know what the truth is! Only truth I know is I don't want to be in here with you ugly dudes.

STEVE

Truth is truth. It's what you know to be right.

VO (INMATE 2)

Nah! Truth is something you gave up

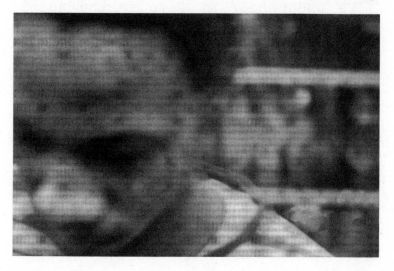

What was I thinking?

when you were out there on the street. Now you talking survival. You talking about another chance to breathe some air 5 other guys ain't breathing.

VO (INMATE 1)

You get up on the witness stand and the prosecutor talks about looking for truth when they really mean they looking for a way to stick you under the jail.

VO (INMATE 3, in a cry for help)

I've spent half my life in the joint, man. Where's my life? Where's my damned life?

We hear the toilet flush as scene ends.

CUT TO: INTERIOR: JAIL. STEVE is dressing for court. We see him checking out his hand, which is slightly swollen.

CUT TO: STEVE sitting in back of van. He holds his hands out in front of his face. They are shaking.

CUT TO: STEVE on stand.

O'BRIEN

Mr. Harmon, did you act as a lookout for the drugstore robbery or check out the store so that a robbery could be safely committed?

STEVE

No, I did not.

O'BRIEN

Mr. Harmon, did you discuss with anyone that you would act as a lookout or that you would check out the store?

STEVE

No, I did not.

O'BRIEN

Mr. Harmon, were you in the drugstore owned by Mr. Nesbitt, the victim, on the 22nd of December of last year?

STEVE

No, I was not.

O'BRIEN

Are you sure in your mind that you know what a lookout would do?

STEVE

Yes, I am.

O'BRIEN

One last question. Were you in any way involved with the crime that we are discussing here? To make it clear—were you, in any way, involved with the holdup and murder that occurred on the 22nd of December?

STEVE

No, I was not.

O'BRIEN

Nothing further.

CUT TO: PETROCELLI riffling through papers. She stops occasionally, looks toward STEVE, and nods. PETROCELLI leans back in her chair and visually confronts STEVE for a long beat. Then she gets up and goes to podium.

PETROCELLI

Mr. Harmon, do you know James King?

STEVE

I know him from the neighborhood.

PETROCELLI

You talk to him much?

STEVE

Once in a while.

PETROCELLI

Once in a while. When was the last time you spoke to him before the robbery?

STEVE

I don't know exactly, but it was during the school year.

PETROCELLI

Didn't you speak to him in December?

STEVE

I don't think so, but I might have.

PETROCELLI

Which is it? You don't think so or you don't remember?

STEVE

Both. I mean, I might have spoken to him, but we don't talk about anything important enough to remember.

PETROCELLI

What do you talk about?

STEVE

Usually I see him in the playground. Maybe he'd say something like "Those guys can't play ball," stuff like that.

PETROCELLI

"Those guys can't play ball." Did you ever see him play ball?

STEVE

I don't remember seeing him play ball.

PETROCELLI

You having trouble remembering what you've seen?

STEVE

No, but I've seen a lot of ball games.
I watch a lot of ball games.

PETROCELLI

Are you nervous? Do you want to take a
few minutes?

STEVE

No.

PETROCELLI

You talk to Bobo sometimes?

O'BRIEN

Objection. We've been referring to the
witness as Mr. Evans.

JUDGE

Sustained.

PETROCELLI

Have you spoken with Mr. Evans?

STEVE

I might have said "Hi" to him. I've

never had a conversation with him.

PETROCELLI

You ever talk to Mr. Cruz? Osvaldo Cruz?

STEVE

Yes, he's about my age. I've talked with Osvaldo.

PETROCELLI

What did you talk to Mr. Cruz about?

STEVE

Same thing, mostly. About playing ball, or the weather. Or what's going on in the neighborhood.

PETROCELLI

Did you hear Mr. Evans's testimony that—let me put it this way—you heard Mr. Evans's testimony that you came out of the drugstore just before the robbery. Is that right?

STEVE

I heard his testimony.

228

PETROCELLI

And are you saying it was just a co-
incidence that you were coming out of
the store at that time?

CUT TO: FLASHBACK of O'BRIEN turning over
the cup.

CUT TO: STEVE on witness stand.

STEVE

I don't know exactly when the robbery
happened, but I know I wasn't in the
drugstore that day.

PETROCELLI

So Mr. Evans was lying?

STEVE

I don't know what he was doing, but I
know I wasn't in the drugstore.

PETROCELLI

You heard Mr. Cruz say that you were
supposed to go in and "check the store
out" for cops. Is that right?

O'BRIEN

Objection! I believe the testimony was that Mr. Cruz was told that was the case.

JUDGE

Do you want the testimony read back?

PETROCELLI

I'll withdraw the question as framed. Mr. Harmon, do you remember Osvaldo saying that he understood you to be the lookout?

STEVE

I heard him say that.

PETROCELLI

And according to you, Mr. Cruz was lying, too?

STEVE

No, somebody could have told him that, but I know I wasn't there.

PETROCELLI

Then he must have lied, is that right?

O'BRIEN

Objection. The prosecution is soliciting an argument.

PETROCELLI

Withdrawn. Mr. Harmon, you say you weren't at the drugstore anytime during the day of the robbery. Perhaps you would tell us where you were.

STEVE

I don't know exactly where I was when the robbery took place. Most of the day I was going around taking mental notes about places I wanted to film for a school film project.

PETROCELLI

Well, if you don't know exactly where you were, can you tell me anyone who might know where you were?

STEVE

I don't even remember where I was. When the detectives asked me where I was, I couldn't even remember the day they were talking about. They didn't ask me about it until weeks later.

PETROCELLI

Then how do you remember——what did you say?——taking mental notes for a school film project?

STEVE

I know that because I was planning to do the film of my neighborhood over the holidays.

PETROCELLI

Getting back to Mr. King. Would you consider yourself a friend of his or an acquaintance?

STEVE

An acquaintance.

232

PETROCELLI

Mr. Cruz, friend or acquaintance?

STEVE

Acquaintance.

PETROCELLI

Mr. Bobo Evans, friend or acquaintance?

STEVE

Acquaintance.

PETROCELLI

So you're acquainted with everyone involved in this robbery, is that—

BRIGGS

Objection! She knows better than that! She knows better than that!

JUDGE

Sustained. The jury will disregard the last question. There is no one who was involved in this affair until the jury makes that decision. And yes, Miss Petrocelli, you do know better.

PETROCELLI (satisfied)

Nothing further.

We see STEVE stand shakily and head back to
the defense table. He looks out onto the onlookers
and sees his parents. His MOTHER forces a smile
and his FATHER makes a fist and nods emphati-
cally. We see STEVE sit down, start to pick up a
glass of water, and have to put it down because
his hand is shaking so badly. O'BRIEN crosses
to the desk and writes on the pad in front of
STEVE. We see what she has written. It says
"TAKE DEEP BREATHS."

O'BRIEN

The defense calls George Sawicki.

CUT TO: CU of GEORGE SAWICKI.

O'BRIEN

Mr. Sawicki, do you know the defendant
sitting at this table?

SAWICKI

I've known Steve for three years. He's
been in my film club.

O'BRIEN

Can you give us your opinion of Mr. Harmon's work?

SAWICKI

I think he's an outstanding young man. He is talented, bright, and compassion-ate. He's very much involved with depicting his neighborhood and environ-ment in a positive manner.

O'BRIEN

Do you consider him an honest young man?

SAWICKI

Absolutely.

O'BRIEN

When he says he was taking mental notes for a film, would that be a film for your club?

SAWICKI

Yes.

O'BRIEN

Nothing further.

CU of MR. SAWICKI. He starts to leave the stand but is then held up by the **JUDGE.**

CUT TO: PETROCELLI.

PETROCELLI

You said you're a teacher in Mr. Harmon's school. Do you live in his neighborhood?

SAWICKI

No, I don't.

PETROCELLI

So although you want to vouch for his character, isn't it fair to say that you don't know what he does when he goes to his neighborhood and you go home to yours?

SAWICKI

No, it's not. His film footage shows me what he's seeing and, to a large extent, what he's thinking. And what he sees, the humanity of it, speaks of a very deep character.

PETROCELLI

What was he doing on the afternoon of December 22nd? Did he show you a film of that day?

SAWICKI

No, he did not.

PETROCELLI

Do you feel that the ability to make a film means that someone is honest?

SAWICKI

It is my belief that to make an honest film, one has to be an honest person. I would say that. And I do believe in Steve's honesty.

PETROCELLI

As a matter of fact you like him quite a bit, don't you?

SAWICKI

Yes, I do.

PETROCELLI

Nothing further.

O'BRIEN

Harmon rests.

BRIGGS

King rests.

CUT TO: STEVE lying on his cot, soaked with sweat. He tries hard to catch his breath. He turns his head to the wall. He lifts one hand and lets it slide slowly down the pale-green wall.

CUT TO: INTERIOR: COURTROOM: CU of JAMES KING. He looks around awkwardly as BRIGGS sums up his defense.

VO (BRIGGS)

So what do we have? We have a man who admits to being part of a robbery accusing another man. And why is he making these accusations? The prosecution would have you believe that bringing Mr. Evans, this "Bobo" character, here, is the result of good police work, which gives Mr. Evans the chance to demonstrate what a great citizen he is. But isn't the truth of the matter that the only reason he's here is

238

because the police have him on a criminal matter, and have offered him a deal if he comes here and implicates someone else? Isn't that the real story?

Does it really surprise anyone that a man who is capable of robbing a drugstore, and he has admitted to doing just that, who then sells the loot from the robbery, and he has admitted to that, and who is caught with drugs, and he has admitted to that—then tries to get a lighter sentence by testifying against another person? Isn't his character, if you can call it character, clear? Hasn't he proven by his own admissions who he is? What he is?

Camera pulls back from POV of JUDGE. We see only MR. and MRS. HARMON on one side of COURTROOM, a few strangers on the other side. The COURTROOM is nearly empty. The camera pans to COURT CLERK, who is going through mail. Then to court STENOGRAPHER, who takes down proceedings. Then to COURT OFFICER, who is nodding, close to sleep.

BRIGGS

What I submit to you, ladies and gentlemen of the jury, is that Mr. Evans made the mistake of selling the cigarettes he stole during the robbery. Did he do the shooting? I don't know. But naturally he says he didn't do it. If he had sat up there on the witness stand and said he did the shooting, he would never have been offered the deal he got. The only way out for him is to look around and find somebody else to accuse. And that's precisely what he did. He could have picked anyone else in the neighborhood. Half the young men of that age group are either unemployed or underemployed. He happened to pick Mr. King.

The State did not produce one witness to the murder. They produced one witness, Miss Henry, who said she saw Mr. King in the store. Where was her mind at the time? According to her testimony, it was on the health and well-being of her grandchild. Could she have made a mistake? Evidently she has. Not that she did not see someone in the store, but whom did she see? She was taken to the police station and given a set of photographs. From these photographs she picked, at police urging, Mr. King. But she didn't pick out this photo from a thousand photographs, or a book of photographs or even 50 photographs. She was shown a handful of photos and asked to pick one. Later, when she had to pick someone from a lineup, what was she doing? Was she picking out the man she saw in the drugstore, or was she picking out the man the police had given her in the photographs? That's for you, the jury, to decide. We heard Mrs. Moore testify that James King was at her house at the time of the incident. Shall we assume that every person who is related to an accused person is going to lie? I don't think so. The prosecution, Miss Petrocelli, paraded in front of you a bunch of admitted criminals, people who have participated in stickups, buying and selling stolen goods, you name it. She has asked you to believe them. Then she asks you not to believe Mrs. Moore, who has never committed a crime in her life. Think about it. If you met these people on the street, which would you believe, which would you trust?

As for Osvaldo Cruz, he is putting as much distance between himself and this crime as possible. All he was supposed to do was to stand outside and push a garbage can in front of a potential pursuer. But there wasn't a pursuer, because Mr. Evans and whoever he was with—if indeed he was with anyone else—made sure of that. And think about this: Lorelle Henry, who seemed for all the world like a decent, law-abiding human being, testified that she was sure that there were 2 men in the store, 2 men involved in the robbery. And we have 2 men who have admitted participation. I submit to you that there's no need to go beyond these two when you look for the perpetrators of this crime. Ultimately, what this case is about is whether you

believe people who are admitted participants in this crime and who are saving
their own hides. If you believe, as I do,
that their positions, their stated characters, so taint their testimony that
everything they say is well within the
area of reasonable doubt, then you have
no choice but to find Mr. King not guilty.
And when you walk away from the sorry
testimony of the State's witnesses, you
have nothing else from the prosecution.
Nothing else. Ladies and gentlemen, at
the beginning of this case the prosecutor spoke of monsters. She not only
found them, but she has brought them here
to testify for the State. I have faith
in you, and faith in the American judicial system. And that faith leads me to
believe that justice in this case demands more proof than you have seen in
this case. I believe that justice demands
that you reject the testimony of these
men, consigning their stories to the
area of deep doubt. I believe that justice demands that you return a verdict
of Not Guilty. Thank you.

CUT TO: POV of JURY. Camera will follow O'BRIEN as she paces from one side of the JURY to the other. Behind her we see the prosecutor's table and the 2 defense tables. Beyond that we see STEVE's MOTHER, sitting on the edge of her seat.

O'BRIEN

First, I would like to thank you for your patience in this trial, and for your attentiveness. It's been clear to everyone involved in this case that you have taken an interest in these proceedings and have brought your minds and hearts to the testimony. I would like to beg your indulgence while I review that testimony.

The most important testimony, the reason we're here, is the Medical Examiner's statement that a murder was committed. A man is dead. But nowhere in the Medical Examiner's testimony does he indicate who was responsible for that murder. That is for you to determine. It is an awesome responsibility. It was testified that the gun belonged to the victim. So we can't trace gun ownership back to the murderer. What can we trace as to the guilt or innocence of my client, Steve Harmon?

The State doesn't even suggest that he was in the store during the robbery. It doesn't suggest that it was his gun that was used. The State does contend that somewhere, sometime, Steve got together with someone and agreed to participate in this robbery. On the stand Steve admitted to having seen Mr. Evans on the street in his neighborhood. Hundreds, perhaps even thousands of people have seen Mr. Evans in the streets of Harlem. Perhaps hundreds of thousands of people. That doesn't make any of them guilty of a crime. The State did elicit from Steve that he spoke to Mr. King about basketball. The conversations were short, and without substance. At no time did the State establish any conversation between Steve and anyone else about a robbery. Think about that for a minute.

Without a plan that says that Steve entered an agreement with the robbers, what would he be charged with? Talking about basketball in the streets of Harlem? Does that now constitute a crime? Not in any law journal that I know about. The State also presents Mr. Evans's testimony that he "understood" that Steve was to check out the drugstore to see if it was clear. Oh, really? The State brought out a witness,

one who everyone agrees has no reason
to lie, Lorelle Henry. Miss Henry said
that she was in the drugstore when the
robbery began. If someone was to make
sure that the drugstore was clear, he
or she made a bad job of it. Remember,
it was the State that proved that the
drugstore wasn't clear. And do you remember the signal that Mr. Evans said
he received? He said that Steven came
out of the drugstore and didn't signal that anything was wrong. In other
words, there was no signal. What is the
significance of this? Well, if there

were a signal, a thumbs-up sign, for example, we might expect someone in the vicinity to have noticed it. Not only did no one without a stake in this case see Steve Harmon giving a sign, Lorelle Henry, a retired librarian, did not see him in the store either. And tell me, how many young black men went into that drugstore that day and walked out without making a signal? Were they all guilty of something?

Do you remember Mr. Evans's testimony that they stopped for a "quick bite" after committing the crime? And who stopped for the quick bite? Do you remember? Let me read to you from the testimony of Mr. Bobo Evans. (O'BRIEN picks up notes, adjusts her glasses, and begins to read.)

Mr. Evans: We took some cigarettes and left.

Ms. Petrocelli: Then what did you do?

Mr. Evans: Then we went down to that chicken joint over Lenox Avenue, across from the bridge. We got some fried chicken and some wedgies and some sodas.

Ms. Petrocelli: Who was with you at this time?

Mr. Evans: Just me and King.

(SHE takes off glasses and looks at jury.) Where was Steve Harmon, the alleged lookout man? Why was there no testimony that Mr. Harmon received part of the loot from this "getover"? The only person we know who profited was Bobo Evans, and we know he made a profit because he sold the cigarettes!

Mr. Briggs has already suggested that the major reason for the testimonies of Mr. Evans and Osvaldo Cruz was self-interest. They were brought here not to answer for their participation, but for the sole purpose of testifying against others. They both understand that the deal they get depends on their convincing you that other people are implicated. Mr. Evans suggests that he

249

believed what the "shooter" told him about someone else checking out the store. But let's look at the reliability of Mr. Evans's testimony. A robbery was committed; a man was brutally killed. The killing here is the key to what these proceedings are about, not the stolen cigarettes, and you understand that. But still Mr. Evans goes around selling the cigarettes that connect him with the crime! Did he think that was a clever move? Or is this a shallow, gullible man who doesn't think about very much of anything? Who among us can watch a man die in a drugstore and then go out for a quick bite a few blocks away? Is this a man whom we can trust to tell the truth about anything? I don't believe him. Do you?

In going over my notes last night, I ran into a question. It's the prosecutor's job to bring all of the participants in a crime to justice, and so Miss Petrocelli has brought everyone she believes might have been involved to this courtroom. But why, if Steven

250

Harmon is innocent, would Mr. Evans want to hurt him? That bothered me quite a bit. But then I thought again about who Mr. Evans was. He had no problem at all in sticking up an innocent man, Mr. Nesbitt. You watched him testify. Did he seem at all bothered by the fact that he had left a man dead? To Mr. Evans, all Mr. Nesbitt represented was a "getover." That's what Steve Harmon is to him as well. Mr. Evans—Bobo—is perfectly willing to leave Steven Harmon lying on a floor or wasting away in a jail cell. The only thing that Steven Harmon is to Mr. Evans is another "getover."

Finally, let us come to the character of Steve Harmon. **(We see O'BRIEN stop and get a drink of water. Then we see her walk next to STEVE.)**

I want you to think about his character as opposed to that of the witnesses for the State. You saw him on the stand. He answered the questions openly and honestly, as would any other young person

of his age. Miss Petrocelli asked him
if he was nervous. Do you remember
that? The implication was that if he
was nervous, it meant that he had something to hide. I submit to you, the
jurors in this case, that you, too,
would have had a degree of nervousness.
He's on trial for his life! He's facing
the possibility of spending his entire
youth behind bars! Under the circumstances I would have been shocked if
he were not nervous. The State paraded
before you witness after witness who,
by their own admission, testified either
to get out of jail or to prevent them-
selves from going to jail, or, in the
case of Mr. Zinzi, to prevent himself
from being sexually molested. Think
of Steve Harmon's character as opposed
to that of Bobo Evans. Compare Steven
Harmon to Mr. Zinzi, another of the
State's witnesses. Compare him to Mr.
Cruz, who admitted taking part in this
crime, who admitted that to become a
member of his gang, he had to slash a
stranger in the face.

Is there reasonable doubt as to Steve Harmon's guilt? I think the doubt was established when Lorelle Henry did not identify Steve as being in the store. It was reinforced with every witness the State brought to the stand.

It's up to you, the jury, to find guilt where there is guilt. It is also up to you to acquit when guilt has not been proven. There is no question in my mind that in this case, as regards Steve Harmon, guilt has not been proven. I am asking you, on behalf of Steve Harmon, and in the name of justice, to closely consider all of the evidence that you have heard during this last week. If you do, I'm sure you'll return a verdict of Not Guilty. And that will be the right thing to do. Thank you.

MS: PETROCELLI from POV of JURY. Behind her we see the prosecutor's table and the two defense tables. We see the two defense lawyers watching intently. Neither STEVE nor KING is directly facing the camera.

PETROCELLI

I would also like to thank you for your attention in this trial. The defense has just given you its version of the facts in this case, and now it is the State's turn.

Let me start by refocusing this case. The defense wants you to go into the jury room thinking that this case is about the character of Mr. Zinzi, who testified that he heard a story about someone who stole cigarettes. It is not about his character. The defense wants you to think that this case is about the character of Mr. Bolden, who bought cigarettes. It is not about his character. The defense wants you to consider the character of Osvaldo Cruz. But this case is not about whether Mr. Cruz is someone we would invite to a party or have as a friend. The defense wants you to dwell on the character of Richard "Bobo" Evans. He is not a nice man, they are saying, and so you should discount his testimony. But this case is

254

not about the character of any of these witnesses. This case is about a crime that was committed on the 22nd of December in which an innocent man, Alguinaldo Nesbitt, was brutally murdered. I don't know what kind of man Mr. Nesbitt was, but I know he did not deserve to be killed in his store, left on the floor while his killers snacked at a fast-food restaurant. This case is not about the characters of Zinzi, Bolden, Cruz, or Evans; it is about Mr. Nesbitt's right to live, and to enjoy the fruits of his labor. It is about the right we all have to life, liberty, and the pursuit of happiness. It is the contention of the State that no one has the right to deprive us of the precious gift of life. It is the contention of the State and it is also the law of the land.

A lot has been said about the motivation of some of the witnesses. They testified, according to the defense, only because they were given a break in their sentencing. Therefore, the defense would have you believe, their testimony is somehow made false. Well, let's reexamine their testimony and find out.

CUT TO: CU of JUDGE. He is taking notes.

CUT TO: MS of PETROCELLI from JUDGE's POV.

Mr. Bolden testified that he received stolen cigarettes from Mr. Evans. We know that the cigarettes were stolen from the drugstore. José Delgado, the drugstore clerk, testified that the cigarettes were stolen. In other words, Mr. Delgado verifies Mr. Bolden's testimony. Did he get a break in sentencing? Or was he simply telling the truth? Did you notice that none of the defense lawyers questioned the character of the clerk or even mentioned it? They want you to forget him.

Mr. Evans testified that he was actually in the drugstore, taking an active part in the robbery. No one has questioned that. He also places Mr. King in the drugstore with him on the 22nd of

December. This testimony was backed up by Lorelle Henry—Lorelle Henry, who had gone to the drugstore to get medicine for her grandchild. Did she get a break in sentencing? Or was she merely telling the truth? When the defense talks about character, they carefully skirt around the character of Lorelle Henry.

Mr. Evans also testified that when he arrived at the scene, he saw Osvaldo Cruz there. This testimony was verified by Mr. Cruz. Yes, I was there, Mr. Cruz testified. Yes, I was part of this robbery. We have three witnesses to the fact that James King was in the store on the 22nd of December: Mr. Evans, Mr. Cruz, and Ms. Henry.

Mr. Evans testified that they did not have a gun but intended to take Mr. Nesbitt's money by force of muscle. He said that Mr. Nesbitt produced a gun that he owned. You heard the City Clerk testify that the gun used to kill Mr. Nesbitt was registered to him. Did the

City Clerk, who verified Mr. Evans's testimony, get a break in sentencing? Of course not. Did the defense attack his character? No, the only thing they could do was to sit and listen to the truth.

Another fact that the defense did not choose to deal with is the sale of cigarettes. The sale of cigarettes to Mr. Bolden, a fact never seriously challenged by the defense, along with the verified theft of cigarettes from the drugstore, also suggests that Mr. King was present in the store during the robbery and murder. Mr. Briggs, the attorney for James King, suggests that Mr. Evans was in the drugstore by himself, or perhaps with Osvaldo Cruz. But Lorelle Henry identified Mr. King as the man she saw in the drugstore. Here is a Black woman, uneasy about her role in identifying a young Black man, who still had the courage to testify before you and to positively identify Mr. King. Mr. Briggs's theory simply does not work. What does work is the State's theory of what happened, verified by all of the witnesses. Mr. Harmon gave the all-clear signal, and Bobo Evans and James King went into the store to rob Mr. Nesbitt. When Mr. Nesbitt tried to defend himself, the gun was taken from him and he was shot by that man, sitting right there **(She points to King.)**, and killed. Ms. O'Brien suggests that if Mr. Harmon had actually cased the drugstore for the robbers, he would have seen Ms. Henry. In other words, he would have been a better lookout man. Well, maybe he hasn't had much experience in helping to rob drugstores. Should we feel sorry for him? For that matter, are Mr. King or Mr. Evans so accomplished in their criminal activities? This was a botched robbery in which the perpetrators actually took very little money and a few cartons of cigarettes. And, oh, yes, the life of a good man, Alguinaldo Nesbitt.

If anybody does not believe that Mr. King was in the store, if they believe that Osvaldo Cruz, Lorelle Henry, and

Bobo Evans are all lying, that the sale of the cigarettes to Mr. Bolden means nothing, then they should find him not guilty. I don't think that is possible. If anybody looking at this case believes that the store was not cased, that Mr. Harmon just "happened" to be at the drugstore, although now he says he doesn't remember where he was, then they should find him not guilty. I don't think that is possible, either. The truth of the matter is that Bobo Evans participated in a crime with Mr. Cruz, Mr. King, and Mr. Harmon.

They are all equally guilty. The one who grabbed the cigarettes, the one who wrestled for the gun, the one who checked the place to see if the coast was clear. What would have happened if Mr. Harmon had come out of that store and gone over to Mr. King and said, "There's someone in the store"? Perhaps they would have gone someplace else to carry out their "getover," or maybe they would have just called it a day and gone home. Steve Harmon was part of the plan that caused the death of Alguinaldo Nesbitt. I can imagine him trying to distance himself from the event. Perhaps, in some strange way, he can even say, as his attorney has suggested, that because he did not give a thumbs-up signal, or some sign to that effect, that he has successfully walked the moral tightrope that relieves him of responsibility in this matter. But Alguinaldo Nesbitt is dead, and his death was caused by these men.

Mr. King's attorney wants to distance Mr. King from the murder by attacking the character of the State's witnesses. But the fact of the matter is that Mr. Evans is an associate of Mr. King. If he had chosen priests and Boy Scouts as his companions, I'm sure we wouldn't be here today. But Mr. King cannot distance himself from the fact—the cold, hard fact—that a man is dead because of him.

Mr. Harmon wants us to look at him as a high school student and as a filmmaker. He wants to think, well, he didn't pull the trigger. He didn't wrestle with Mr. Nesbitt. He wants us to believe that because he wasn't in the drugstore when the robbery went down, he wasn't involved. Again, perhaps he has even convinced himself that he wasn't involved.

But yes, Mr Harmon was involved. He made a moral decision to participate in this "getover." He wanted to "get paid" with everybody else. He is as guilty as everybody else, no matter how many moral hairs he can split. His participation made the crime easier. His willingness to check out the store, no matter how poorly he did it, was one of those causative factors that resulted in the death of Mr. Nesbitt. None of us can bring back Mr. Nesbitt. None of us can restore him to his family. But you, you twelve citizens of our state, of our city, can bring a measure of justice to his killers.

And that's all I ask of you: to reach into your hearts and minds and bring forth that measure of justice. Thank you.

CUT TO: EXTERIOR: COURTROOM. The doors of the court are closed as the camera nears it. The door is pushed open and we see the INTERIOR of the COURTROOM. We see the JURY turned toward the JUDGE, who speaks in a quiet, almost fatherly manner. We hear his voice as the camera seems to settle down on a seat. STEVE, sensing that a friend has arrived, turns and tries to smile at MR. SAWICKI but cannot manage it through his nervousness.

We look around the COURTROOM as the JUDGE's voice drifts in and out.

JUDGE

If you believe that Mr. King was a participant in the robbery, whether he actually pulled the trigger or not, you must return a verdict of Guilty. If you believe . . . (Voice fades out.)

CUT TO: Stuart portrait of George Washington on right wall.

CUT TO: New York State flag. Then: American flag.

CUT TO: Motto over desk.

JUDGE

. . . that Mr. Harmon did go into the store with the purpose of . . . (Voice fades out.) without regard to who actually pulled the trigger . . .

CUT TO: Wall mural.

CUT TO: JURY.

CUT TO: CU of JUDGE.

JUDGE

Then you must return a verdict of Guilty of felony murder.

Camera, from POV of STEVE's MOTHER, swings wildly around the room, stopping momentarily at those symbols that fill the COURTROOM. Throughout this time the last words of the judge are repeated.

JUDGE

Then you must return a verdict of Guilty of felony murder.

Then you must return a verdict of Guilty of felony murder.

Then you must return a verdict of Guilty of felony murder. . . .

FADE OUT.

FADE IN: STEVE in CELL. For the first time JAMES KING is in the cell with him. KING leans against wall, still dressed in the clothes he wore at the trial.

KING

How you doing? You scared?

STEVE

Yeah. You?

KING (subdued)

Naw, ain't nothing to it. If the man wants you, he got you. Ain't nothing to it, man.

GUARD

Hey, we got a pool going. I bet you guys get life without the possibility of parole. The guys on the next block think you're going to get 25 to life. You guys want in on it?

CUT TO: STEVE. He looks away, then buries his face in his hands.

CUT TO: GUARD. He is smirking.

GUARD

That a yes or a no?

CUT TO: Two YOUNG MEN, handcuffed together, being led to the next cell. One looks terrified. The other is putting on a show of bravado.

GUARD

You guys treat me nice, and I'll put in a word for you up at Greenhaven. Maybe I can get you a boyfriend that's really built.

CUT TO: STEVE in the MESS HALL. He avoids looking at KING. There is a shoving match down from where he sits. An inmate reaches over and takes STEVE's meat with a fork. STEVE looks up and sees the taker looking at him menacingly. He looks down at the tray.

CUT TO: STEVE in CELL. Outside the cell there is a clock on the wall with a wire guard over it. The second hand moves slowly.

CUT TO: INMATES enjoying a domino game as if they are far away from the prison, in some friendly setting.

Friday afternoon, July 17th

Last night I was afraid to go to sleep. It was as if closing my eyes was going to cause me to die. There is nothing more to do. There are no more arguments to make. Now I understand why so many of the guys who have been through it before, who have been away to prison, keep talking about appeals. They want to continue the argument, and the system has said that it is over.

My case fills me. When I left the courtroom after the judge's instructions to the jury, I saw Mama clinging to my father's arm. There was a look of desperation on her face. For a moment I felt sorry for her, but I don't anymore. The only thing I can think of is my case. I listen to guys talking about appeals and I am already planning mine.

Every word that has been said in court is burned into my brain. "Steve Harmon made a moral decision," Ms. Petrocelli said. I think about December of last year. What was the decision I made? To walk down the streets? To get up in the morning? To talk to King? What decisions did I make? What decisions didn't I make? But I don't want to think about decisions, just my case.

Nothing is real around me except the panic. The panic and the movies that dance through my mind. I keep editing the movies, making the scenes right. Sharpening the dialog.

"A getover? I don't do getovers," I say in the movie in my mind, my chin tilted slightly upward. "I know what right is, what truth is. I don't do tightropes, moral or otherwise."

I put strings in the background. Cellos. Violas.

GUARD

King! Harmon! You got a verdict! Let's go!

CUT TO: COURTROOM, now fairly crowded. O'BRIEN is talking to JUDGE. She finishes and sits down next to STEVE.

O'BRIEN

They got a verdict this morning. They've just been waiting for the Nesbitt family to arrive.

STEVE

What do you think?

O'BRIEN

They have a verdict. I hope it's one we want to hear. No matter what it is, we can continue your case. We can appeal. You okay?

STEVE

No.

JUDGE

Is everybody here? Is everybody here?

CLERK

I think so.

JUDGE

Prosecution ready?

PETROCELLI

Ready.

JUDGE

Defense?

CUT TO: CU of O'BRIEN.

O'BRIEN

Ready.

CUT TO: CU of JUDGE.

JUDGE

Bring in the jury.

Very LS as WORDS roll slowly over the screen as in the beginning.

This is the true story of **Steve Harmon.** *This is the story of his* **life** **and of his** **trial.**

(We see the jury members taking their places in the jury box.)

It was not an episode that he expected.
It was not the life or activity that he thought would fill every bit of his soul or change what life meant to him.

(The JUDGE has read the verdicts and hands them to the CLERK as GUARDS stand behind the DEFENDANTS.)

He has transcribed the images and conversations as he remembers them.

The color begins to fade as the JURY FOREMAN reads verdicts. Two GUARDS begin to put hand-cuffs on JAMES KING as color changes to black and white. It is clear that the JURY has found him guilty. We see KING being taken from the COURT-ROOM.

We see JURY FOREMAN as he continues to read.

CUT TO: CU of STEVE's MOTHER. We see her desperately clasping her hands before her, her face distorted with the tension of the moment, then suddenly, dramatically, she lifts her hands high and closes her eyes.

CUT TO: The GUARDS who were standing behind STEVE move away from him. He has been found not guilty. STEVE turns toward O'BRIEN as camera closes in and film grows grainier. STEVE spreads his arms to hug O'BRIEN, but she stiffens and turns to pick up her papers from the table before them.

CUT TO: CU of O'BRIEN. Her lips tense; she is pensive. She gathers her papers and moves away as STEVE, arms still outstretched, turns toward the camera. His image is in black and white, and the grain is nearly broken. It looks like one of the pictures they use for psychological testing, or some strange beast, a monster.

The image freezes as last words roll and stop mid screen.

A Steve Harmon Film

December, 5 months later

It is five months since the trial, almost a year, minus a few days, since the robbery in the drugstore. James King was sentenced to 25 years to life. Osvaldo was arrested for stealing a car and sent to a reformatory. As far as I know, Bobo is still in jail.

My mother doesn't understand what I am doing with the films I am making. I have been taking movies of myself. In the movies I talk and tell the camera who I am, what I think I am about. Sometimes I set the camera up outside and walk up to it from different angles.

Sometimes I set the camera up in front of a mirror and film myself as a reflection. I wear different clothes and sometimes try to change my voice. Jerry likes to use the camera, and I let him film me, too. Whatever I do pleases my mother, because I am here with her and not put away in some jail.

After the trial, my father, with tears in his eyes, held me close and said that he was thankful that I did not have to go to jail. He moved away, and the distance between us seemed to grow bigger and bigger. I understand the distance. My father is no longer sure of who I am. He doesn't understand me even knowing people like King or Bobo or Osvaldo. He wonders what else he doesn't know.

That is why I take the films of myself. I want to know who I am. I want to know the road to panic that I took. I want to look at myself a thousand times to look for one true image. When Miss O'Brien looked at me, after we had won the case, what did she see that caused her to turn away?

What did she see?